CELEBRITIES AND CHAOS

CINDY BELL

ISBN-13: 978-1548673154
ISBN-10: 1548673153

CONTENTS

CHAPTER 1

Mary tugged open the door of the dryer and caught the warm sheets that spilled out. It seemed to her that she couldn't get the laundry done fast enough. Dune House was filled to the brim, and keeping up with the housekeeping was a little overwhelming, but she loved every minute of it.

"Here, let me help you with that." Suzie stepped into the laundry room and took half of the sheets. "Crazy, isn't it?"

"Yes." Mary laughed as she followed Suzie out of the laundry room and into the hallway. "Fun, but crazy."

"Are you holding up okay?" Suzie paused in front of one of the guest rooms. "If you need a break, just let me know."

"I'm fine, Suzie, I promise." She winked at her friend then disappeared into one of the rooms. As she changed the sheets she couldn't help but glance around the room. It was filled with assorted memorabilia, both from the television show that was currently being filmed in Garber, and other hit shows that the guest had taken part in. Ty Hobbs was a popular reality TV actor and presenter, and although Mary hadn't seen many of his shows, she knew that he was quite well-known. It was easy to be impressed by him, as he was handsome, but also quite gregarious. He'd had everyone laughing over dinner the night before. She smoothed down the sheets and as her hand ran underneath one of the pillows, it bumped into something hard and smooth. She drew her hand back and stared at the pillow. She suspected what it was, but didn't know what to do.

"Excuse me, I didn't realize you were in here." Ty paused in the doorway.

"Sorry, yes, just putting on fresh sheets." She glanced over at him with a nervous smile.

"Thanks." He stepped inside the room and looked over at the bed. "The pre-breakfast meeting finished early, I can take it from here."

"Sure." Her hands fluttered for a moment, she

had no idea what to do with them, however as he walked past her towards the bed, she clasped them behind her back and summoned up strength. "Ty, we don't allow weapons in Dune House."

"Weapons?" He looked over his shoulder at her. "What do you mean?"

"Well, I was putting on the sheet, and I had to go under your pillow and…"

"This?" He laughed as he picked up the pillow and revealed a metal cylinder, that to her had felt like the barrel of a gun. "It's my toothbrush. I hide it here because the members of my crew like to play pranks on me. You would not believe the places I've found it." He rolled his eyes. "They all think it's funny, but I got tired of replacing it."

"I see, I'm so sorry." She flushed as she realized she'd just wrongly accused a celebrity.

"It's quite all right, just do me a favor and keep my secret, hmm?" He winked at her then hid the toothbrush under the pillow again.

"Yes, of course I will." She stepped back out of the room and tried to forget the embarrassing moment. However, the more she tried not to think about it, the hotter her cheeks became. Luckily, she didn't have time to dwell on it as there were other sheets that needed to be changed. She hurried into the next room, and went down the line until she ran out of sheets. There she ran into Suzie again.

"All done." Suzie breathed a sigh of relief. "Now, we just have to get breakfast on the table."

"And we'd better hurry." Mary glanced at her watch. "They have to be on set by ten."

As they reached the bottom of the stairs that led into the kitchen, six people filed in through the front door. They were additional staff and crew. Since all the rooms at Dune House were full they had been set up at the local motel, but were still invited to partake in the meals at Dune House. Suzie grabbed some eggs from the fridge while Mary greeted the guests and inquired what they would like to drink. By the time breakfast was on the table, Suzie was exhausted, and ready to eat. They all squeezed around the long wooden table in the dining room. The chatter was so loud that Mary could only smile at Suzie from across the table, there was no chance to actually converse. When a couple came in the door, late to breakfast, Mary jumped up.

"Hi Cynthia, Marcus, please come and join us."

"Sorry we're late." Cynthia shot a look of displeasure towards her husband, then settled at the table.

"Let me get your breakfast." Mary stepped into

the kitchen. Cynthia was the only member of the crew that ate a vegan diet, so she kept her breakfast separate from the rest. When she returned with a fresh baked muffin, a bowl of fruit, and her favorite sparkling water, Cynthia was caught up in a conversation with Ty.

"I just think if we really push it today we could wrap up a day or two early. But if you keep letting everyone slide, then we're going to run behind."

"I get that, but it's not up to me, you know that. The director has the final say on whether a scene is complete, and if he wants to do retakes, we need to do retakes." He paused a moment and pushed his egg around on his plate. "Maybe, if you and I rehearsed a few of the scenes again, I'd be able to nail it better."

"You have plenty of people you can rehearse with." Marcus crossed his arms as he studied Ty. "She already works long hours."

"It's not work, Marcus, it's helping out Ty, and besides, we want to be finished on time, right?" She shot a smile in her husband's direction. "If this is the way we get to that, then why complain?"

"Right." He narrowed his eyes, but didn't say another word. He looked down at his plate and left his food untouched.

"Here you go, Cynthia." Mary set the breakfast down in front of her.

"What is this?" She looked at the muffin, then picked up her fork and poked it.

"It's a cinnamon raisin swirl muffin. I thought you might like it." Mary smiled. "I baked it this morning."

"And did you use egg in this muffin, or milk?" She raised an eyebrow.

"No, of course not."

"And I guess you completely overlooked the fact that I am gluten free?" She crossed her arms.

"What?" Mary blinked, her heart began to pound. "I don't recall that being on the list of your meal requirements."

"I'm sure it was there, since I've been gluten free for over a year. Is it safe to assume that you used flour in this muffin?" She shoved her plate away.

"Well yes, but I didn't know." Mary frowned. "I can get something different for you. Let me take that away." She reached for the muffin.

"No!" Cynthia slapped it out of her hand. "The whole plate of food is ruined, anything might have been contaminated. I don't understand how this place got such great reviews for good customer service when you could have made me ill with the breakfast you tried to serve me. Take it away I said!"

Mary stared crestfallen at the muffin on the floor. She'd taken extra time to bake it just for Cynthia, and the scent of it had nearly driven her crazy with hunger. Now, no one would be able to eat it.

"Excuse me, that's quite enough." Suzie started to stand up.

"No, it's all right, Suzie, it's all right." Mary bent down to pick up the muffin and did her best to ignore the pain in her knees and back. The aches just reminded her that she had about thirty years on the woman who bossed her around. Maybe it was customary for Hollywood types to be so ruthless, but she certainly wasn't used to it. She carried the breakfast back into the kitchen and looked back at the list that Cynthia gave her. Sure enough, in tiny print all the way at the bottom were the words 'gluten free'. She closed her eyes and shook her head. In her younger days, she doubted that she would have missed that. But as it was, she often had a difficult time reading fine print. It made her feel awful that she really had made a mistake, and that Cynthia could have possibly fallen ill due to it. However, she was also certain that the woman could have been more gracious about it. She prepared a new bowl of fruit, and paired it with the cereal that Cynthia deemed acceptable on her list. Then she added the almond milk that she requested. As she carried it back to the table, the conversation had died down. Some of the guests had already left, while others were just finishing up. She placed the bowl down in front of Cynthia.

"Here you are, I'm so very sorry about the mistake."

"It's too late now!" She huffed as she stood up from the table. "It's almost ten o'clock, I can't eat this now. What is wrong with you?" She turned and stalked out of the dining room.

"I'm sorry, she's under a lot of stress." Marcus frowned as he watched her go. "She's just a little wound up."

"No, it was my mistake, it's all right." Mary cleared her throat and did her best to hold back tears. She was humiliated by the woman's behavior, and also felt responsible for the terrible mistake. "I'll make sure her lunch is perfect."

"Trust me, with Cynthia, nothing is ever perfect." He rolled his eyes, then followed after his wife. The show's producer, Drake, wiped his mouth and stood up.

"I have to get going. Thanks for the breakfast, ladies."

Ty stood up as well and winked at Mary. "Chin up, darling, she's not actually gluten intolerant she just wants to lose ten pounds."

Mary's cheeks flushed at his words, with anger. Was she really throwing a tantrum over a diet? It made her infuriated to think so. Ty was already out the door before she could find the words to express what she felt.

"What a piece of work, huh?" Suzie rolled her eyes as she began to clear the table.

"Yes, quite." Mary stared at the door. "One of these days someone is going to knock her down a peg, then we'll see how she handles it."

"No, we won't." Suzie picked up another plate. "Because you and I won't ever have to see that woman again by the end of this week. Keep that in mind."

"Good reminder." Mary nodded.

❧

Twenty minutes later, the house was empty of guests, and the kitchen was quiet but for the sound of the faucet filling the dishpan. Mary sank her hands deep into the soapy water and smiled to herself as the warmth eased some pain in her fingers and wrists. She dreaded mentioning her aches and pains to the doctor, but she knew that one day soon she would need to.

"Let me help with that." Suzie rested her back against the counter beside her.

"No, it's fine, I enjoy doing the dishes." Mary shrugged as she began to wash a plate.

"You aren't overwhelmed by all of this?" Suzie frowned as she glanced over the quiet kitchen. "Sometimes I wonder if I made a mistake by agreeing to host all of these people."

"No way, you didn't make any mistake." She looked up at her with a wide grin. "I'm loving this. Having a house full of people, and taking care of them, it just feels right."

"I'm glad you think so." Suzie kicked off one shoe and reached down to rub her heel. "All the running back and forth is making muscles ache that I didn't even know I had."

"It sounds like you need a walk on the beach." Mary nudged her with her elbow. "Go on, I've got this. Go clear your head."

"Are you sure?" Suzie met her eyes. "I don't want to leave all of the work to you."

"Don't worry, I'll get you back later when the floors need to be mopped."

"Ugh." Suzie laughed. "Deal." As she stepped out through the back door, she noticed that there were many boxes and crates piled up near the shed. She knew that the crew had stored some things there, but didn't realize how much. It amazed her how much went into a production. She'd always watched television shows, but she'd never really thought about the amount of work it took to produce them. Even the crew was much larger than she expected. As she began to shift the boxes into the shed, she heard a voice from the side deck of the house. It wasn't hard to hear it, as it sounded as if the person was quite angry.

"I don't care who invited her. I am supposed to be warned if she is going to be part of the crew, so why wasn't I contacted? That is what I want to know." He paused as if he was waiting for a reply, then raised his voice even more. "That is your job. You are supposed to know these things. No, I don't want off of the crew, are you kidding me? This is the best chance I have at being a presenter again someday. But you'd better believe that if she says one word to me, we're going to have trouble."

Suzie cringed as she heard those words. She

didn't know who the person on the phone was, or who he was angry at, but she guessed that they might both be guests at Dune House. That much anger trapped in one space was not going to end well. She made a mental note to look into it, maybe there was something she could do to ease the tension. As she set the last box in the shed, she didn't hear the man's voice anymore. She guessed that the conversation was over, and hoped that he would calm down. She closed up the shed then headed down to the beach. It was a beautiful morning, and although one part of the beach was roped off for filming, the view was still glorious and the environment serene.

The day she'd received a call from the producer, Drake, requesting to rent out all of the rooms in Dune House, she'd thought it was a joke. Now and then they received wealthy guests, and sometimes well-known ones, but she'd never considered hosting an entire television crew, let alone Ty Boggs. She'd almost hung up, when he insisted that since they received a permit from the town of Garber to film their pilot for a new TV show on a nearby segment of the beach, they thought Dune House would be the ideal location. As the show was on a limited budget, he had requested that Suzie and

Mary cater for all of the crew and actors as it was cheaper than getting a catering service.

Suzie wasn't sure if they could handle the influx of guests and catering for so many people, but decided it was time to find out. Now that they were in the middle of it, she still wondered if it might have been too much, not just for them, but the entire town. She'd heard complaints from some of the local businesses that the stars and crew were quite demanding, and expected to be catered to in ways that the small town was not familiar with. However, with only days left in filming, and the amount of revenue it generated for the town, she hoped that it would turn out to be a positive thing. The further she walked along the beach, the more relaxed she became. Though, there was a time in her life when she craved being in the middle of all of the action, now she found solace in the small town, and the beautiful beach that bordered it. When her cell phone rang, she jumped at the sound, then smiled at the sight of Paul's name.

"Hi honey, are you home?"

"Yes, just pulled in a little while ago. I have some things to do on the boat, then I'll be free. I'm guessing that you won't be though." He chuckled. "Can you use an extra set of hands?"

"You just want to try to get some autographs, don't you?"

"Not a chance. Unless you're offering yours."

"You can always have mine." She smiled and savored the sound of his voice. Paul was a professional fisherman. He had just returned from a long trip and she was looking forward to spending some time with him. "Come on by whenever you're free. We'll be there."

"Okay love, until then." He hung up the phone.

She tucked the phone back into her pocket and took a deep breath of the salt-filled air. Maybe things were a little chaotic, but what could possibly disrupt paradise?

CHAPTER 2

When Mary glanced at the clock, she realized it was close to lunch time. She already had most of the food prepared for the day. When Suzie returned from her walk, they'd carted some of it down to the catering tables near the set. Now that she'd gone off to pick up some things from town, Mary decided to take the last of the items down herself, along with the perfect lunch she'd prepared for Cynthia. She just hoped it would make up for the horrible breakfast.

Once she had everything piled into bags, she started across the sand. As Mary neared the ropes along the beach, she felt a bit of a rush carry through her. She'd never been one to idolize celebrities, but somehow being part of the process, even if it was just providing lunch, seemed exhilarating.

She watched as the camera crew rolled along the sand and filmed the conversation between two actors. It was easy to see the strain in their muscles, and just how much precision it took to make sure that the camera was angled just right. However, as the scene came to a close, the director stood up from his chair and threw down his clipboard.

"Garbage!" The shriek that carried across the otherwise calm beach drew the attention of everyone within earshot. "I told you we need seriousness in this scene! Was that a giggle? Was it Ryan?" He snatched up his clipboard and waved it through the air. "How am I supposed to film this if you can't give me what I'm asking for?"

"Preston, I think he's just a little nervous, maybe if we do a few more dry runs?" Cynthia offered in a soft tone from a few feet away.

"Excuse me?" He snapped around to look at her. "Was anyone talking to you?"

"I'm sorry, I just think that if you take it easy, Ryan will respond better to your direction." She placed her hands on her hips. "Clearly, the intimidation tactics aren't working. Look at him." She pointed to the young man, who appeared to tremble where he stood. "You can't replace him now, so you're going to have to figure it out, or we're all just wasting our time here, Preston, and you know it."

"You don't ever tell me what to do." He stomped over to her and glared straight into her eyes. "You are nothing, do you hear me? A mere consultant. You baby these people too much, that's the problem. You're so soft on them that they think their opinion matters. It doesn't. They are cattle!" He shouted his last words.

"Uh, maybe we should take a break. I'm sensing we have some hangry people around here." Ty looked straight at Mary. "You've arrived just in time."

"Oh sure, take a break, never mind that time is money. Never mind that we haven't gotten past this one scene all morning. Let's all just stuff our faces." Preston threw his clipboard down again, then turned and walked away. Mary nervously walked over to the refreshment table and made sure that everything was ready. It wasn't long before it was almost wiped clean. She noticed that Cynthia hung back. She appeared to be speaking with Ryan, though it didn't seem as if her efforts were reassuring to him. Since Mary brought her a special vegan meal she decided to walk it over to her while it was still fresh. As she approached she caught the tail end of their conversation.

"I got you this job, that doesn't mean that you can act like this. I told you, Preston is hard to work for. I warned you. So straighten up or I will find a way to replace you!" She turned to storm away, but nearly walked into Mary instead. "What?" She shouted.

"I'm sorry, I just thought you might like your lunch before it gets cold." Mary took a step back, startled by the force of the woman's voice.

"Fine." She snatched the box from her hands. "This better be edible."

"I'm sure you will like it, it includes a warm quinoa salad. I double-checked your list, and made sure to use only the ingredients on it. I do hope this will help to make up for breakfast." Mary offered her the warmest smile that she could muster.

"I doubt it." Cynthia rolled her eyes and stalked away.

"Nice." Mary shook her head and turned to walk back towards the refreshment table, when she heard her name spoken from just behind her. She turned to see a young man. She struggled to recall his name, but couldn't place it. "Yes?"

"I couldn't help but overhear. I'm Shawn." He offered her his hand.

"Shawn, that's it. Sorry, I just couldn't think of it." Mary smiled and shook his hand. "Did you have enough to eat?"

"More than enough. I've been grazing from that table. Thanks for all of the effort you put in. And, I'm sorry she treated you that way." He frowned. "She can be so difficult to work with. Trust me, I know from experience. I wish she wasn't on this production at all. But Ty insisted."

"I'm sure she's just under a lot of pressure." Mary waved her hand. "I guess it's not unusual for people in show business to be a little demanding."

"Maybe a little, but she takes it to a whole new level." He sighed and glanced back at the roped off area. "I have to get back. Just try not to let her get to you."

"Thanks for the advice." She met his eyes with a small smile.

"If you have any trouble at all, just ask for me, all right?" He patted her shoulder. "You've done a great job for all of us, really, I mean that." He turned and headed back towards the production area.

Mary watched him for a moment longer, then walked back up the beach towards Dune House.

~

*A*s humiliated as Mary was by Cynthia's tantrum, she was also left questioning herself. Could she do a better job? She certainly didn't want something she did wrong to cause a bad review of Dune House that might be read by hundreds of people. She vowed that she would make an effort to behave more professionally and to stay away from everyone during production. When she reached Dune House she decided to check on the towel supply in the bathrooms before she started to prepare dinner. She was on the last bathroom when she heard the front door open, followed by some voices.

"Really, Marcus I'll be fine. Just go back to work. I need to lay down, that's all."

"I can stay with you if you want."

"No! So you can get fired from another production? I swear sometimes it seems like I'm the only one that cares about all of the bills we need to pay. If I thought I was going to be sick before, now I really feel sick. Get out!"

Mary jumped as she heard heavy steps on the stairs. She stepped out of the bathroom as Cynthia reached the hallway.

"Cynthia, excuse me." She stepped to the side. Cynthia barely looked at her as she stormed towards Drake's room.

"Drake said I could rest here, I'm not feeling well." She slammed the door shut without ever looking at Mary.

Mary shook her head and continued down the stairs. Whatever was eating Cynthia, she guessed, was better left alone. To calm her nerves and ensure some quiet for Cynthia, she decided to step outside and straighten up the porch. She lost herself in thought as she turned and brushed off each cushion, then wiped down the arms of each of the chairs. She spent some time sweeping off the porch until she realized she was just pushing the same few grains of sand back and forth. She set the broom against the house and took a deep breath as she looked out over the water. She knew she had to find a way to let go of everything she was starting to bottle up. She didn't want to carry resentment towards Cynthia, but she also knew she wasn't the type of person she would like to spend a lot of time around. When she heard Suzie's car pull into the parking lot, she was relieved. She always had a way of making things clear to Mary, no matter how complicated they seemed.

"Mary, how is your afternoon going?" Suzie smiled as she mounted the porch and walked towards her friend.

"Honestly, I'm a little flustered. I had a run-in with Cynthia at lunch time." She frowned as she met Suzie's eyes. "I hope it doesn't cause any problems."

"What kind of run-in?" Suzie pulled out one of the chairs at the table and sat down.

"She wasn't happy about me interrupting her. I just wanted to give her the lunch I made her, since she wasn't happy about the breakfast I made." She sighed and shook her head. "She was already wound up about something, and I should have known better. Anyway, now she's upstairs in Drake's room resting because she's feeling sick. I guess maybe that was why she was so short with me."

"Ah, that's possible. We should check in with her later to see if she needs to see the doctor. I'm sure he'd be willing to come out for a visit." Suzie glanced at her watch, then back at Mary. "We should get dinner going as we're going to have a hungry crew arriving soon."

"Yes, you're right." Mary straightened out the

extra chairs along the wall. She reached for the doorknob, but before she could turn it, a loud scream rattled the glass. Her heart dropped at the sound, as it wasn't just any scream, but a deep primal scream that made the hairs on the back of her neck stand up.

"What is it?" Suzie pushed past her and pulled the door open. "Drake? What is it?" She froze just inside the door as she caught sight of Drake crouched down on the floor near the stairs.

"She's dead!" He rocked back on his heels and moaned. "She's dead!"

"Who's dead? What are you talking about?" Suzie's voice faded as she stepped through the kitchen and into the dining room. There, crumpled at the bottom of the stairs, was Cynthia. "Call an ambulance, Mary! Now!" She rushed forward and shooed Drake out of the way to check Cynthia's pulse.

"No, she's gone." Drake wiped at his eyes, but it didn't stop the flow of tears. "Nothing can be done."

Ty came through the door and ran straight towards Cynthia when he saw her body. "What's happened?" He sunk to his knees beside Cynthia.

"Suzie, is she breathing?" Mary kept her phone pressed against her ear.

"No." Suzie closed her eyes. "It's too late."

"What?" Mary's eyes widened.

"She's dead, Mary!" Suzie looked up at her with wide tear-filled eyes.

The phone dropped out of Mary's hand. As it clattered to the floor she could hear the operator calling out to her for information. But what could she say? She didn't want to tell her that she'd been out on the porch the entire time, while Cynthia drew her last breaths. In the distance she could hear sirens. But she knew that the arrival of the police, and an ambulance, would do nothing to change the reality before her. Cynthia was dead, the same woman she'd just been frustrated with, the same woman that had been so dissatisfied with Mary's service. An immeasurable amount of guilt carried through her as scenarios of how she might have been able to save the woman played through her mind.

CHAPTER 3

The front door burst open and Jason, followed by two paramedics, rushed inside. Suzie stepped away from Drake and Ty as Jason gazed down at the body on the floor.

"What's happened here?" Jason looked straight at Suzie, while the paramedics surged past him to check Cynthia's pulse.

"I'm not sure. Maybe she fell down the stairs?" Suzie glanced up at the stairs. "They aren't very steep. Maybe she slipped?" She looked back down at Cynthia.

The paramedics confirmed that there was no sign of life. Jason spoke into his radio to summon backup.

"We're going to have to investigate this so we can determine what caused her death." He looked from Suzie to Mary. "We're going to have to search the property."

"Anything." Suzie nodded. "Anything that's needed to figure out what happened here."

"Oh, poor Cynthia." Mary cupped her hand over her mouth and tried not to burst into tears.

"Who was the last one to see her?" Jason spun in a slow circle as he looked between the four faces.

"Drake is the one who found her." Suzie placed her hand on his shoulder. "We came in when we heard him scream."

"But I found her like this." Drake wiped at his eyes. "I just wanted to check on her between takes. She said she was feeling ill and was going to rest on the porch. I told her to go ahead and use my room. I can only think whatever was making her sick, caused her to pass out, or maybe fall down the stairs."

"I was coming to check on her as well." Ty struggled to hold back tears. "Maybe if I'd come sooner."

"I guess, I was the last one to see her." Mary's voice wavered as that realization dawned on her. "I was replenishing the towels in the bathroom upstairs when she came in. I heard her arguing with her husband, and then he left. When she walked past me, she said that Drake had offered his room to rest in."

"That was it, nothing else?" Jason stared into her eyes. "This is the most crucial time, Mary, if someone did harm her, your memory will be the freshest right now. Did anyone else come into Dune House after she arrived?"

"I honestly don't know. I went outside, and I stayed outside, until Drake found her." Mary clenched her hands into fists at her sides. The very thought of Cynthia at the bottom of the stairs while she wiped down deck chairs and swept off the porch made her feel terrible. Why hadn't she just gone in to check on her? Usually, her nurturing nature would have demanded it.

"You didn't hear anything suspicious? She didn't cry out when she fell down the stairs?" Jason made a note in his notebook as more police officers arrived.

"No, I didn't hear anything." Mary closed her eyes as a wave of guilt washed over her. "How could I not hear anything?"

"It's all right, Mary." Suzie hugged her, and looked over at Jason. "That's enough, she's told you everything that she knows. This is a big shock."

"I know it is." Jason turned his attention to Drake. "You said she was feeling ill?"

"Yes, right after we started filming again, after we stopped for lunch. She said she was dizzy and sick to her stomach. She thought maybe the sun had gotten to her. So I sent her back here to rest."

"She has a room here?" Jason glanced between the four.

"No." Mary frowned. "She was staying at the motel."

"I didn't want her to drive or walk all that way when she was feeling sick. That's why I suggested she use my room here." Drake looked away as officers began to assess the area around Cynthia's body. "I should have walked with her."

"Did anyone go with her?" Jason looked over at Mary. "You said you heard her arguing with her husband?"

"Yes. They came in the door. I didn't see them, but I could hear them, because they were a bit loud. He said something about staying with her, she refused and told him to go back to work or he'd be fired. I'm sorry, I don't remember exactly. But that was the general idea." She shivered and stepped aside as another officer brushed past her and began to take photographs.

"Did you actually see her husband leave?" Jason looked towards the door, then back to her.

"No. I heard the door shut though."

"Are you certain?" He held her gaze.

"I..." She frowned. "I don't know. I thought I did. I'm sorry, Jason."

"It's okay." He patted her shoulder. "Just try to relax. I know that it's difficult, but anything you can tell me will be useful."

"There's nothing else to tell."

"Maybe we should step outside." Suzie bit into her bottom lip. "We'll need to inform the other guests."

"Not just yet." Jason nodded his head to Summer as she entered through the front door. "Summer's here to try to determine the cause of death. Once she does then we can decide on our next steps."

Suzie watched as Summer walked over to Cynthia's body. She was certain that it had to be an accident. What else could it be? She'd ended up at the bottom of the stairs, and was in the house all alone, so there was no other explanation that she could think of. When she put her hand on Mary's shoulder, she could feel how much her friend's body trembled.

"It's all right, Mary, all of this will be over soon. What a terrible thing to happen." She took a deep breath and looked into Mary's eyes. "No matter what, you couldn't have done anything to prevent this. I know that's what you're thinking."

"Oh Suzie, I just can't believe I was right outside." She shuddered and turned into her friend's embrace. "I should have checked on her, or made her some tea, or some soup."

"Sh. Don't torture yourself."

"Jason." Summer looked over at him with a grim frown. "Can I speak to you, please?"

"Sure." He walked towards her. Suzie started to follow after, but Summer shook her head.

Suzie froze. The look in Summer's eyes left her with an empty feeling.

"Suzie, what is it?" Mary looked past her at Summer. She and Jason leaned their heads close together and spoke in quiet tones. Jason looked up, then over at Suzie and Mary. He paused, then pulled out his radio and said something into it. With deliberate steps he walked back over to them.

"I'm sorry to tell you, but this death has been ruled a homicide."

"A homicide?" Mary gasped. "But how? Does

Summer think someone pushed her down the stairs?"

"Actually, there is no indication that she fell down the stairs. She may have collapsed at the bottom. However, there are signs that she was poisoned."

"Poisoned?" Suzie's eyes widened. "By what?"

"Most likely something she ingested, though there will have to be more testing to determine exactly what and how. For now, the entire house is going to have to be roped off and scoured for the source of the poison."

"But, where will all of the guests go? How long will it take?" Suzie's mind raced as she tried to put together all of the information that Jason gave her.

"It may take up to a few days. Everything will need to be processed. All of the guests, and the two of you will have to be interviewed. Do you know if she ate anything recently? Anything from the kitchen?" He looked over at the kitchen, then back to them.

"From our kitchen?" Suzie gazed at him with wide eyes. "There couldn't be anything in our kitchen that would have poisoned her. Mary and I do all of the cooking and all of the grocery shopping."

"Oh no." Mary's cheeks flushed. She looked down at her hands, which were clasped tight in front of her.

"What is it, Mary?" Jason peered at her. "Do you have something to tell me?"

"It's just." She took a deep breath, then released it slowly. "I took her lunch. Out on the beach. I'm not sure if she ate it or not, but I took it to her."

"What was in it?" Jason began jotting down notes on his notepad.

"Wait just a minute." Suzie placed her hand on Mary's still clasped hands. "Nothing Mary made could have been poisoned. Jason, I know you have to do your job, but…"

"You're absolutely right, I have to do my job, and as far as I know Mary was the last one to give her food, and the last one to see her alive, so I will be asking her questions." Jason's brow furrowed as he looked at Suzie. "A woman is dead, I can't take any chances here, or offer any favors."

"Of course you can't, Jason," Mary mumbled. "I wouldn't expect you to. I'll give you the recipe I used, it lists all of the ingredients. But of course, as far as I know there was nothing unusual in it." She walked into the kitchen, her mind a fog as she sorted through her recipe cards. Was it possible?

Did something poisonous slip into the food she'd prepared? She couldn't imagine how. She kept a clean kitchen, and rarely left food unattended. What could possibly have gotten into the food that would kill a person? "Could it have been a food allergy, Jason?" She handed him the recipe card.

"No. I don't think so. Summer would be able to tell the difference. Thanks for this. Listen, I know this is going to be hard on both of you, but trust me, it will be much better in the long run if I conduct a thorough and air tight investigation, understand?"

"Yes." Suzie frowned as she crossed her arms. "But that doesn't mean I have to like it."

"Do you two have somewhere to stay?" He studied them.

"I guess we'll go to the motel. There should be enough room there for the rest of the guests, too. I'll just grab a few things." Suzie started in the direction of the hallway.

"No, I'm sorry." Jason winced as he put his hand on her arm. "I can't allow you to remove anything from the property. Not until everything has been processed."

"Not even our clothes? Our toothbrushes?" Mary stared at him.

"No, nothing. Once everything has been

processed you can retrieve it. It's the only way we can be certain that there is nothing in the home that could have caused Cynthia's death."

"Cynthia?"

Suzie looked up at the sound of another voice. Marcus stood in the doorway.

"Marcus." She started towards him.

"Cynthia!" He ran forward and shoved Ty out of the way as he stood up to console him. "What did you do to her?"

"Me?" Ty stammered and took a few steps back. "I didn't do anything. She was like this when I got here. Drake found her like this. I'm sorry, Marcus."

"No! This can't be happening!" Marcus covered his face with his hands and moaned. "We were going to work things out, we were. What happened?" He dropped his hands and looked straight at Suzie. "What happened to my wife?"

"Sir, I'd like to speak with you." Jason drew him off to the side.

"I'm going to call the motel and make arrangements for everyone. We're going to have some very unhappy people on our hands." Suzie stepped out onto the porch as she dialed the number of the motel. She could see that there were more members of the crew headed in the direction of the house.

How would they react to the news of Cynthia's death? She guessed that they wouldn't be pleased to find out that they wouldn't be able to take any of their belongings with them to the motel. Once the arrangements were made she faced the daunting task of informing the guests that gathered on the porch.

"The situation we are faced with is a tragic one. I know that many of you will be grieving, and I am so sorry for your loss. While the police are investigating Cynthia's death, we will need to move to the motel. Once the bed and breakfast is released from the investigation you will be able to collect your things and if you choose to stay, you can of course."

"Wait, are you saying we can't get anything from the house?" Shawn stepped forward, his eyes wide.

"I'm afraid not, not just yet. But I can assure you that the moment the contents of the bed and breakfast are released, we will be informed first. Mary and I will be moving to the motel as well, and if there's anything we can do for any of you while we are there, please feel free to contact us."

"This is terrible." Shawn frowned.

"Has anyone told Preston?" Ty looked around the group of people. "Has anyone called him?"

"I don't think so." Shawn shook his head. "He's

going to be furious. I doubt that he'll postpone the shoots."

"I'll talk to him." Ty crossed his arms.

"Everyone, listen once more please." Jason stepped out onto the deck and looked around at the crowd. "We are going to need to question you, it shouldn't take long, but I do need you to be available for questioning and stay in Garber until otherwise advised. I do hope that you will cooperate with the investigation, so that we can get justice for Cynthia's murder."

Among grumbles, there were a few nods of agreement. Suzie did not envy Jason's task of weeding through all of their last moments with Cynthia, but she hoped he would find something out quickly.

CHAPTER 4

*A*fter Jason cleared the guests to leave, Suzie and Mary headed over to the motel. It was a strange procession of cars, trucks, and equipment vans that paraded down the main street of Garber. After picking up some essentials they headed on to the motel.

When they arrived at the motel several of the staff members were outside to greet them. Suzie and Mary slipped away to their room.

"At least here we might have some privacy." Suzie sighed as she closed the door behind her.

"Oh Suzie, what are we going to do?" Mary turned to face her, just as there was a knock on the door.

Suzie jumped and turned to face it.

"Who could that be?" She grabbed the knob and

pulled the door open to find Paul on the other side. "Paul, come in." She stepped aside as he walked in. Mary sank down at the foot of one of the beds.

"I came as soon as I heard." He looked between Suzie and Mary. "Are you two okay?"

"I'm not sure." Mary shook her head and scooted forward on the edge of the bed. "I just keep replaying those last few minutes."

"You're going to drive yourself crazy, Mary." Suzie sat down, swept her close to her and gave her shoulder a squeeze. "Paul, it's awful. I just can't believe this happened. I have no idea how long Jason is going to have Dune House shut down."

"You could always stay with me."

"Thank you, Paul, but I think it's better if we stay here. Even though our guests are staying here now, they are still our guests. The moment that Jason releases Dune House we'll be able to move them all back in."

"Those that want to go back." Mary frowned and looked towards the door. "I'm not sure that any will."

"Trust me, they would much rather be at Dune House than here." He peered at Suzie. "Any idea what really happened?"

"Just that she was poisoned. We have no idea by

who or with what." She frowned as she tightened her grasp on Mary. "As far as we know Mary was the last one to see her alive."

"I'm sorry, Mary." Paul met her eyes. "This must be very hard for you."

"I have to admit that the hardest part is knowing I'm a suspect." She closed her eyes.

"I know that has to be very unnerving." Paul paced slowly across the room. "I just hope that we're able to figure out what happened here, and fast."

"Hopefully, Jason will get to the bottom of things quickly." Suzie stood up and joined him as he paced. "As soon as we know how Cynthia was poisoned that should help point things in the right direction."

A knock on the door made Mary jump. A part of her, despite knowing that what happened to Cynthia was not her fault, still expected to be arrested. Why not, when she had been just a few feet away as a woman died?

"Are you expecting anyone?" Paul glanced at them.

"No, but it could be one of the guests. I told them they could reach out to us if they needed anything." Suzie started for the door, but Paul opened it before she could reach it.

"Wes, I'm glad you're here." Paul offered his hand, but Wes pushed past him and headed straight towards Mary.

"Mary, I'm surprised you didn't call me." He met her eyes and then embraced her. "Why didn't you?"

"I'm sorry." She rested her head on his shoulder. "I know how busy you are, and I didn't want to distract you from that case that you've been working on."

"You should always feel comfortable calling me, Mary, especially when something like this happens. That is what I'm here for. I had no idea until I heard from Jason." He pulled back enough to look into her eyes again. "I don't want to be the last one to know."

"I'm sorry," Mary murmured as she was comforted by his presence.

"Jason called you?" Suzie raised an eyebrow. "Why?"

"He has requested assistance from Parish PD, for the investigation. Our toxicology experts are often tapped by other departments as we have the best resources in the area. Given the fact that this murder will get lots of attention, he would want to make sure all bases are covered and it is solved as quickly as possible." He slipped his hand into Mary's. "When I found out what happened, I came straight here. Are you okay?"

"Yes." She smiled some as she squeezed his hand. "I'll be fine. Once this is all worked out. I can't believe she was poisoned."

"Listen, Mary you need to consider getting a lawyer." He released her hand then pulled out his wallet and began to thumb through it. "I know of a very good one."

"A lawyer?" She laughed, then shook her head. "No, I don't need a lawyer."

"You do, and you will get one." He looked up from his wallet and straight into her eyes.

"Don't be silly, Wes." She saw a level of forcefulness in his gaze, as if he wouldn't take no for an answer. "If I hire a lawyer it will just make me look guilty."

"Mary, I have read the write-up on the case so far, and you are the prime suspect."

"Prime suspect?" A wave of dizziness washed over her. Luckily, Wes was there to steady her. "Are you certain?"

"Yes, I am. I can't tell you more than that. Throughout the investigation I won't be able to help you, Mary, that's why I want you to hire a lawyer." He searched her eyes. "Why put yourself at risk?"

"I have no intention of putting myself at risk, Wes. But I'm not going to even entertain the idea that I might be convicted of a crime that I didn't commit. What will everyone think when they find out that I've hired a lawyer? I'll tell you what they'll think. They'll think I have something to hide." She shook her head. "No, I'm not ready for a lawyer. At least not yet. If things get more serious, you can let me know, and I'll hire a lawyer then."

"No, I can't." He shoved his wallet back into his pocket. "You're not hearing me, Mary. I can't even communicate with you, not much anyway, while all of this is going on. I could risk tainting the case with my personal relationship with you."

"But Jason sometimes keeps Suzie informed…"

"I am not Jason and under the same circumstances he wouldn't give Suzie any information. My boss already knows about our relationship, and he has warned me that he will be watching me like a hawk. I'm sorry, Mary, but the best I can do is tell you to hire a lawyer, and clearly you're not interested in listening to my advice." He frowned. "I will do everything I can on my end to try to make sure the investigation is accurate, but I can't influence it."

"I wouldn't ask you to." She stared at him with wide eyes. "In fact, you should probably go. I'm sure you're not supposed to be here."

"I'm not." He leaned close and kissed her cheek. "Promise me you'll be careful, Mary."

"I will be." She frowned as she watched him turn on the heel of a cowboy boot and walk out of the room. He barely shot a look in Paul and Suzie's direction, then closed the door behind him.

A deep silence filled the room the moment that Wes left. Suzie looked over at Mary with concern.

"Are you okay, Mary?"

"I can't believe that he won't help me." Mary stared at the closed door.

"It's not that he doesn't want to, Mary, it's that he can't." Paul frowned as he leaned back against the door. "I know it's hard to understand, but if he's caught interfering in a case, he could lose his badge over it."

"Wes' whole life is about being a cop." Mary sighed and looked down at her hands. "I guess I can understand why he wouldn't be able to help me."

"We don't need his help anyway." Suzie flipped her brassy-blond hair away from her eyes. "We can take this into our own hands. First, we need to figure out who the actual suspects are."

"Yes, you're right." Mary nodded. "Do you have anyone in mind?"

"Well really, as of now, everyone is a suspect." Suzie rubbed the back of her neck as she considered the options. "Everyone on the crew, everyone staying at Dune House, everyone in town."

"And me." Mary piped up with a sigh. "Don't forget about me."

"Sweetie, you're the only one that I won't even consider as a suspect." Suzie sat down beside her.

"What about me?" Paul raised an eyebrow. "I didn't do it." He raised his hands in the air.

"I know you didn't." Suzie laughed. "Thanks for lightening the mood though."

"Is that what I did? I was just worried that you might think I was a killer." He winked at her.

"The problem is there's nothing funny about it." Mary shook her head. "I want to smile and laugh, but I keep thinking of Cynthia."

"Of course you do." Suzie leaned close to her. "It was quite a shock to see her there."

"Yes. It must have been terrible for Drake." She cringed as she recalled the tears in his eyes. "He really seemed to care about her."

"Not to mention Ty. He looked devastated."

"You know Shawn mentioned to me that Ty

asked for her specifically to be on the show. He said that if Ty hadn't done that, Cynthia never would have been here. I bet Ty feels guilty about that now."

"Shawn told you that?" Suzie tapped her chin. "I wonder how he knew so much about it?"

"Shawn doesn't seem to like her one bit. In fact he seemed upset that she was working on the crew."

"Oh, wait a minute." Suzie's eyes widened. "I bet he was the one I heard on the phone, arguing with someone. It was after she got upset with you at breakfast. He seemed irate that someone was working on the crew, but I never put two and two together about who it might be."

"You think it was Cynthia?" Paul stepped forward. "That might be motive right there."

"Do you think he would murder Cynthia just because he didn't want to work on the same crew as her?" Mary shook her head. "That doesn't make much sense to me."

"No, but maybe there was more to it than we know." Suzie narrowed her eyes. "I'm going to look into Shawn and see what I can find out about him."

"Right now, we need dinner, and then some rest." Paul glanced at his watch. "The Chinese place around the corner is still open. I'll grab us all something to eat. What would you like?"

"Thanks Paul, but I don't think I can eat." Mary rubbed her hand across her stomach. "I already feel sick."

"Mary, you have to keep your strength up. If we're going to get through this, you're going to need your wits about you. We all are. Just order something, even if you don't eat it now, we can keep it in the mini-fridge for later. All right?" Suzie asked.

"All right." Mary nodded. As they placed their orders, her stomach flipped again. She felt so awful that she could almost believe she was poisoned as well. Only the poison that filled her belly wasn't fatal, it was filled with guilt and uncertainty.

Suzie pulled out her phone and began looking up information about Shawn Blunder. She remembered his full name from the registration paperwork.

"Oh, wow." She raised an eyebrow. "He does have quite a social media presence, both his own, and people speaking about him. He doesn't have too many fans it seems. Some of the comments are downright cruel, and border on threats."

"It's strange, he was nice to me. Kind even. I would say he went out of his way to comfort me. I wonder why so many people think differently about him?" Mary peeked at the screen of the phone.

"I'm not sure, I'm trying to sort through all of the colorful language to get to actual information. Oh, here we go. This person says that Shawn's documentary ruined his life, and that he should be in jail for fraud. Ouch." She glanced up at Mary. "Do you know anything about this?"

"No." Mary's eyes widened. "I haven't heard anyone else mention it. What exactly did he do?"

"All I know is there are mentions of the information in his documentary being false, and that some people lost jobs, and their reputations because of it."

"I bet he would tell me if I asked him. He seemed eager to talk before. Maybe I should try to strike up a conversation with him? What do you think?" She looked at Suzie nervously.

"I think it's a good idea. And the sooner the better. If he did do this, then he's not going to be talkative if he thinks anyone suspects him."

"Well, I don't suspect him. He might not have liked her, but the way he spoke to me, made me think he's a respectful young man. I don't think he would have hurt her."

"Perfect, then you should be the one to talk to him." She glanced back at her phone. "I just got a text from motel management that they are hosting a dinner for everyone in the lobby. Too bad Paul already went to get the food!"

"Yes, but maybe Shawn will be there. I'll go see if I can catch him."

"I'll go with you." Suzie started to stand up.

"No stay, I don't know how long I'll be and Paul doesn't have a room key. You two eat without me, like I said, I'm not hungry."

"Okay, I'll make sure yours gets in the fridge."

As Mary left the room, Suzie looked back at her phone. She continued to sort through all of the rants that were posted about Shawn. Maybe Mary thought he was a nice guy, but it seemed as if she might be in the minority.

CHAPTER 5

*M*ary made her way quietly down the hallway. Her muffled footsteps on the carpet still sounded loud to her keenly trained ears. If someone whispered something somewhere, she wanted to hear it. Not only because she wondered what they might think of her, but also because they might be confessing to a horrible crime. Who killed Cynthia? The question played on her mind as she continued into the lobby. It was drowned out by the sound of a large group of people. Just about everyone from the motel was gathered in the middle of the lobby around buffet style tables. The rest were scattered among tables, chairs, and couches. After a few seconds of skimming faces, she spotted Shawn mixed in with the large group of people. He wasn't hard to spot as several people faced him, and all seemed to be arguing with him. As she drew closer she could hear the heated exchange.

"You keep quiet. She's dead now, there's no reason to keep spreading rumors."

"They're not rumors, and I have every reason to. Do you think it's funny to find a note like this under your door?" Shawn held up a piece of paper, that Mary squinted to read.

I know what you did. Murderer.

Her heart skipped a beat. Apparently, Suzie wasn't the only person that suspected him.

"So what if someone put that under your door? Of course, everyone thinks you had something to do with it. I know you were trying to convince Preston to throw her off the set." Marcus's jaw twitched as he glared at him. "Don't act innocent now."

"Of course I tried to get her off the set. You know she's not supposed to be working anywhere near me. You of all people should be glad she's dead..."

"Shut your mouth!" Marcus pulled his hand back to punch Shawn, but a man beside him grabbed him before he could.

"Enough!" Ty's voice cut through the din and drew the attention of everyone in the lobby. "This is not how this crime is going to be solved. Shouting matches and throwing punches will only make more work for the police and the people of this town. We are still guests here, aren't we?" He looked between Marcus and Shawn. "Leave it."

"No problem." Shawn straightened his collar, then stalked off towards the tall front window that overlooked the parking lot. The tension in the room was thick, but under Ty's steady gaze, the crowd dispersed. Mary was relieved that he was there to break things up before they got too messy.

"Shawn, are you okay?" Mary walked over to him as he separated from the larger group of people.

"Yes, I'm fine. Everyone is just a little tense, I understand it." He frowned as he glanced over at her. "How are you holding up?"

"Not so well." She sighed as she glanced nervously back at the crowd, then to him again. "I just keep thinking about Cynthia, and how innocent she was."

"Innocent?" He laughed, a deep and long laugh that shook his entire body. "I can assure you, there was nothing innocent about her."

"Shawn." She frowned. "You shouldn't talk that

way about her. She's gone now, it's best to think of her positive qualities."

"Being dead might be the only positive quality she's ever had." He crossed his arms and started to walk away.

"Shawn, wait." Mary placed her hand gently on his arm and drew him back. "I'm sorry, I shouldn't have been so quick to judge. You seem like such a nice person, she must have done something to really hurt you for you to feel that way about her."

"You're right. She did. Before I met Cynthia, I was a good person. At least, I thought I was. I was someone that would never wish harm on anyone, no matter how horrible. But after I met her, I learned that there are some people on this earth who make it their mission to torment you. I trusted her, and she stole from me. She ruined my entire future, and thought that she could just laugh it off as an innocent mistake. But I knew the truth, she had a plan, and she thought she would be able to take everything from me. Instead, we both lost everything. But I was the hardest hit, my reputation will never be the same."

"Why don't you tell me what happened? I have a good ear for listening. We certainly have plenty of time on our hands, don't we?"

"Yes, we do." He scratched the curve of his cheek. "But I'm not sure that you would really want to hear this story. It's a bit much to take in."

"I would." She searched his eyes. "Maybe it will ease the burden that you carry even just a little if you share with me. It's worth a try, don't you think?"

"No, it will only place a burden on you to hear me whine about things that are in the past. As you said, she's dead. There's nothing more she can do to me now, and there's nothing she can do for me either. Maybe if she lived long enough she would have come around and asked for my forgiveness, but I doubt it. She didn't seem like the type to ever ask for forgiveness."

"I'm sorry you had such a rough time of it with her. What exactly happened?" Mary searched his eyes for any hint of the truth. She sensed that his intention was to dodge her questions, but she thought if she asked enough times he might provide her with at least a clue of what happened between himself and Cynthia.

"It's best not to talk about it. Anything I say can and will be used against me, as we've just witnessed." He tipped his head towards the crowd. "It's pretty clear that Marcus thinks I was involved in his wife's death, which is pretty amusing, since he is the one that should want to murder her. Good luck, Mary." He looked into her eyes one last time, for longer than necessary, then turned and walked away. She gazed after him, more confused than ever. She could understand why Marcus thought that Shawn had killed his wife, but why would Marcus want her dead?

~

Suzie's eyes hurt from reading all of the comments, some of them were terrible. She was relieved when she heard a knock on the door.

"Suzie, it's me Paul, open up. These boxes are hot."

"Just a second." She rushed to the door and opened it. "Oh, that smells delicious. Thanks so much for getting it, Paul."

"No problem. I'm starving, too. Where's Mary?" He carried the boxes over to the small table near the mini-fridge.

"She went to see if she could speak with Shawn. We both think that he might have been involved somehow. Or at the very least, he was upset with Cynthia for some reason. Yum, egg rolls."

"Yes, there are plenty. Do you think she's okay alone out there?" He frowned.

"I'm sure she is. Mary may seem timid, but she can really handle herself, and when she is determined, she is determined."

"Hmm, sounds familiar." He smiled as he pushed her container across the table to her. "Did you find out anything more?"

"Not really, but I did read the most recent news release about Cynthia's death. Word has traveled fast, they've already announced that she was poisoned. I can only imagine that this is going to make Jason's job even harder."

"Yes, it probably will. But it's going to be nearly impossible to keep a lid on things. Cynthia might not have been well-known, but her death occurred during the filming of a show with popular celebrities. I'm surprised that this town isn't covered in press already."

"Actually, the report didn't mention the location. I'm willing to bet that Preston is going to an awful lot of trouble to ensure that the location of the set is not revealed. If people flock here to spy on the case, then it might make it impossible for Preston to finish filming."

"Good point. I guess he has more influence than I thought."

Suzie smiled before taking a bite of her food. When the door swung open, she looked up to see Mary. "You two missed a near fist-fight in the lobby." She dropped down on the edge of her bed.

"Oh? Who was it?" Suzie turned to face her.

"Shawn and Marcus." Mary sniffed the air. "Oh, that smells really good."

"You should eat." Suzie pointed to the container on the table. "It's still warm."

"Yes, I think I might." Mary joined them at the table. As they shared the meal she recounted the information Shawn had given her. "Unfortunately, I still don't know exactly what happened between them, but the animosity he feels towards her is clear, and he's not even attempting to hide it. I think he's too angry to pretend that he isn't."

"That definitely sounds like motive." Paul finished the last bite of his food. "Is there anyone else that you think might know the truth?"

"Maybe Ty." Suzie closed up her container and stuck the leftovers in the mini-fridge. "He and Cynthia seemed close, right? And Ty insisted on having her on the set, even though he knew there were issues."

"Yes, you're right." Mary snapped her fingers. "I'm sure he would know what's going on. And he's the one that broke up the fight. He seems pretty involved in Cynthia's world. But it's too late to catch him tonight."

"You're right." Paul glanced at his watch. "I should be going, too. Call me if anything comes up, otherwise I'll be here for breakfast in the morning. You two are not alone in this."

Mary offered a small smile. She was glad that Paul was so eager to be involved, but it stung a little as she was reminded of Wes' absence.

After Suzie returned from walking Paul to the car, she settled in her own bed. A second later, she looked over at Mary. "So, what do you think Shawn meant when he said that Marcus should want to murder Cynthia?"

"I'm not sure." Mary looked over at her through the dim lighting. "But we should definitely find out."

"I'm sorry, Mary." Suzie's voice softened.

"Sorry for what?"

"That you're caught up in all of this. I keep thinking there might be something I can do to make sure that you're not a suspect in this investigation.

I've tried to talk to Jason but he's not taking my calls or texts. Summer isn't either." She frowned. "I know they are married and Jason being my cousin means they have to be extra careful about the case, but it's so frustrating not to know exactly what's going on."

"Yes, I haven't heard a thing from Wes since he left earlier this evening. But Suzie, you're already doing everything you can do, by trying to find the real killer. Besides, I'm sure my name will be cleared soon enough. I have the truth on my side, and that usually wins, right?"

"Right." Suzie's whisper didn't sound convincing as it barely broke through the silence in the room. As both women tried to fall asleep, uncertainty filled the space between them.

Mary turned over in her bed and tried to force out all of the worrisome thoughts. But the moment she pushed one away, five more popped up. It was so easy to assume that everything would be fine, but what if it wasn't? What if she ended up in hand-cuffs, and behind bars? The very thought made her shiver. But, she reminded herself, that simply couldn't happen. It was impossible. Wasn't it?

Suzie listened for the sound of Mary's subtle snoring. When she didn't hear it, she knew her friend was still awake. Which meant she was worried. Which worried Suzie, too. Her stomach churned, and she doubted that it was from the Chinese food. It was a scary situation, there was no getting around that. She pulled the blanket tighter up to her chin and squeezed her eyes shut. Maybe, just maybe, she would wake up in the morning and find out the case was solved overnight. She could hope.

CHAPTER 6

*E*arly the next morning, Suzie woke from a wicked dream. In it she chased after Mary, who ran in a panic down a long unsteady bridge. No matter how loudly she tried to call out to Mary, the words never left her lips. When she woke up sweat covered her brow. She did her best to breathe as she fought her way out from under the blanket. For several seconds she had no idea where she was. The dark motel room was far different from the bedroom she was used to waking up in. As reality settled in around her she realized that Mary's subtle snoring drifted through the air. As she climbed out of bed, she did so quietly. If Mary needed anything, it was rest. But she couldn't possibly go back to sleep, not after that dream, that still echoed through her senses. She knew the motel's coffee bar opened early and hoped that she might run into someone else who had trouble sleeping.

After dressing, Suzie stepped out into the silent hallway. She guessed that there weren't too many early risers. When she reached the lobby she found it was almost empty, aside from Ty, who stood in front of one of the coffee pots.

"Good morning, Ty." She stepped up beside him to pour herself a cup of coffee.

"Good morning, Suzie." He glanced over at her. "I'm sure this is pretty difficult for you, being displaced this way."

"Yes, it is. But it's a small price to pay if the police are able to find Cynthia's killer."

"You're right, it is." He carried his coffee towards one of the tables. "Would you like to join me?"

"Yes, thank you." She added some cream and sugar to her coffee, then settled at the table with him.

"So, what has you up so early, Suzie?" He ran his finger along the screen on his phone, preoccupied with whatever was on it.

"I like the peace that early morning can offer."

She watched as he flicked his finger across the screen.

"I run in phases. Sometimes I have insomnia then I sleep whenever I can."

"Do you have it now?"

He looked up from his phone, almost as if he'd forgotten she was there, and nodded.

"I do. I got about two hours last night."

"I guess, all of this is difficult to process. I can't imagine what it must be like for you when you have to deal with your public image as well as the personal tragedy of the loss of a friend." She raked her gaze over the small reactions on his face, and as she expected, tension rippled along the lines of his lips and the crease of his brow.

"It is difficult. I've known Cynthia for a long time. She played a role in my success." He tucked his phone into the pocket of his suit jacket, then looked across the table at her.

"She did have some problems though, didn't she? Something with Shawn? I heard about the scuffle last night between him and Marcus. You broke it up?" She met his eyes.

"Yes, things got a little out of control. Marcus is upset, of course, and Shawn, he's a target because of his past with Cynthia."

"What can you tell me about Shawn?" She noticed that his face tensed again with that question.

"Shawn?" He rubbed a hand across one eye, then looked at her. The exhaustion was etched into his skin with more pronounced wrinkles and dark circles under his eyes. He seemed to have aged overnight. "He's a good guy, a solid crew member, but I don't know him too well personally."

"You said he had some trouble in the past with Cynthia? Do you know anything about that?" She picked up her cup of coffee and took a sip.

"I don't know." He sighed and stared down into his own cup. "I heard some rumors. Okay, I heard more than that." He grimaced. "The truth is that Cynthia made a pretty big mistake with him. Some people claimed it wasn't a mistake, it was intentional. But I don't think Cynthia would ever do something like that."

"What kind of mistake could have been so bad that there are rumors about it?" She raised an eyebrow.

"A few years ago, Shawn was the hottest thing in ground-breaking documentaries. He was about to break on to the scene with a controversial documentary, so hyped up that tickets were sold out for the first three showings before the film was even completed. I mean, it was crazy." He chuckled, and shook his head. "There wasn't a single person in film that didn't know his name. It would have launched his career, and he would have had his choice of directors and other producers to work with. However, that's not how it went."

"What happened?" She turned the coffee cup between her palms and did her best to appear casual, but her heart pounded in her chest. It sounded like plenty of motive for murder.

"Cynthia was in charge of vetting and verifying the stories that were presented in the documentary. Shawn insisted that she be very thorough as he didn't want anything to come back on him in the long run. He had a lot of belief in the subject matter of the film, which is why he gave the job to someone else. He felt he couldn't be as impartial as he needed to be. However, not a day after the film was completed a news story broke about it, that claimed several of the people in the documentary were telling fake stories, and backing them up with fabricated evidence. As you can imagine, Shawn was upset, and supposedly when he confronted Cynthia she didn't have a good explanation. I don't know the exact details, all I know is that Shawn had to pull the film, he lost all of the money that he invested and even though there were at least some true stories involved, the entire subject matter became suspect because of the scandal surrounding the documentary."

"Wow, poor Shawn." She frowned. "I can only imagine how heartbroken he must have been."

"Yes, he was ruined." Ty cleared his throat. "I can understand why he'd still be angry. I hate to think it, but it's possible he had something to do with this. I mean, if I were to point a finger at someone, it would likely be him. How could he not be looking for revenge?"

"I guess he would be." She sighed, then took another sip of her coffee. "What was the documentary about?"

"It had to do with genetically modified organisms and chemical toxins in produce. He claimed to have validated proof that some of the fruits and vegetables being sold in grocery stores were actually poisoning..." He gasped as the word slipped past his lips.

"Poisoning people?" Suzie met his eyes, and held them. "His documentary was about people being poisoned?"

"Well, I mean, not with actual poison. But with

chemicals." His voice trailed off. "I'm sure that's just a coincidence."

"It might be. It might not be." She stood up from the table and picked up her cup of coffee. "Thanks for your time, Ty. Again, I'm so sorry about your loss."

"Thank you. It's still hard for me to believe." His cheeks flushed as he closed his eyes. She guessed that emotion was about to overwhelm him, and could sense that he wanted to be alone. As she walked away her mind raced with the information about Shawn. It seemed to her that he had plenty of motive to seek revenge on Cynthia. He'd already lost everything, it might not matter to him to lose his freedom, too.

~

*W*hen Suzie returned to the room, Mary was already awake and dressed.

"Hey, I was about to send out a search party." She smiled.

"Sorry, I woke up early, and then I ran into Ty in the lobby. He had some interesting things to say about Shawn."

"Oh?" Her eyes widened. "What things?"

Before she could answer there was a knock on the door. Suzie jumped, as she was only a few inches away from it. When she opened it to find Jason and Kirk, she felt a wave of relief.

"Jason, what's the update?" Suzie smiled as he stepped through the door.

"Uh, ladies." He pulled his hat off his head and held it tight in his hands. "I'm going to have Kirk ask you a few questions."

Kirk stepped in just behind him. He already had his notepad in his hands, and although Suzie smiled at him, he didn't smile back.

"Why is that?" Mary looked between the two with an apprehensive stare.

"Because, I think it would be best if he interviewed you. He can be more impartial than I can." Jason cleared his throat, then placed his hat back on his head. "Kirk will tell you everything that you need to know. I'm going to go speak to some of the other members of the crew."

He stepped back out through the door before Mary could say another word to him. Alone with Kirk, it seemed as if all of the oxygen was sucked out of the room. Kirk was a nice enough man, but he took his job very seriously, and as Jason had implied, he was not as close to Suzie or Mary.

"What is this about, Kirk?" Suzie crossed her arms and settled her gaze on him.

"Actually, I need to speak to Mary alone." He glanced up from his notepad. "Would you mind stepping out, Suzie?"

"Yes, I would mind actually. I would mind very much." She moved in front of Mary. "Anything you have to ask Mary, you can ask in front of me."

"Suzie, it's okay." Mary took a deep breath. "I'm sure that whatever Kirk needs to talk to me about can all be cleared up. I have no problem with cooperating with the investigation."

"But, Mary..."

"Great." Kirk flashed a brief smile. "Suzie." He opened the door for her.

"Unbelievable," Suzie muttered under her breath as she stepped out through the door. She turned back to say something else, but Kirk pushed the door closed before she could speak.

Inside the room, Mary wrung her hands together and did her best to keep her composure.

"It's bad, isn't it Kirk?" She stared at him with wide eyes.

"As of now, we are certain that Cynthia was

poisoned by something that she ate. There was nothing accidental about it, Mary." He studied her with such scrutiny that she shivered at the pressure of his gaze. "As I understand it you had a confrontation with Cynthia twice before she died. Is that true?"

"Well yes. I'm not sure I would call them confrontations, but there were two incidents."

"Can you describe those incidents to me?"

"I don't think either was a very big deal, but yes I can." She recounted the issues Cynthia had with her breakfast, and then her reaction to Mary interrupting her with her lunch. "She was quite upset with me. But I understood that she was just frustrated, and I overstepped by interrupting. As for breakfast, that was my fault, it was an honest mistake, but it was my fault."

"So, you didn't intentionally prepare her food that she was allergic to?"

"Oh, she wasn't allergic to it, she was just on a diet." She shrugged.

"So, because you thought she wasn't allergic to it, you decided to prepare her something with gluten?"

"What?" Mary blinked. "Absolutely not." She stood up from the edge of the bed and frowned. "I would never do something like that. No, she had written it very small at the bottom of a long list of things she could not eat, and I just overlooked it. My eyes aren't what they used to be you know."

"So, your eyesight is failing?" He made a note on his notepad. "Then it might have been possible that you picked up something other than what you intended to use? Say, maybe some rat poison?"

"What?" She laughed, then shook her head. "No, absolutely not. First of all, I would never store poison anywhere near food, and secondly I can see just fine. She just wrote it very small, and I wasn't paying attention."

"So, you did serve her food that she expressly asked you not to?"

"Yes, but not on purpose." She sighed and gazed at him. "Why don't you just get right to the point, Kirk? There's no reason for us to do all of this back and forth."

"Okay, well the point is, you were the last one to prepare her food, and from what we know the last one to see her. We're still waiting on the results from her stomach contents, but I think it's pretty safe to assume that you were the most likely person who could have put something into her food. Since you had a problem with Cynthia, maybe you decided that you would do something to upset her stomach. Maybe you didn't know that it was going to poison her. Maybe you thought it would just be funny, she would feel sick, get an upset stomach, as payback for being so rude to you. I'm sure it was an innocent mistake. You put in too much, or she had a much stronger reaction to the poison than you expected."

"Are you serious?" She narrowed her eyes and took a step towards him. "Kirk?" As she searched his stern expression, her heartbeat quickened. "Oh, my goodness, you are!" She clasped a hand over her mouth, then shuddered. "You can't really think I would ever do such a thing, can you?"

"I only think what the facts tell me to think, Mary. The facts say that you had access, motive, and the knowledge to be able to poison this woman. Just fess up now, tell me what kind of poison you used, and I'm sure that we can turn this into a case of accidental death. I mean, I'm sure you didn't set out to kill her." His voice softened as he studied her. "This can all go much easier if you just tell the truth."

"I did nothing of the kind!" Each word she spoke sounded like a shriek to her own ears. Her heart pounded, her face burned with a mixture of anger and embarrassment, and she could barely catch her breath. "I would never harm anyone, and would certainly never poison anyone. You have your facts backward, young man, and if you ever accuse me of anything so horrible again I will make sure that you learn your lesson."

"Oh?" He stared at her, his eyes cold, and his brows knitted tight. "Are you threatening an officer of the law? That's quite the temper you have there. If someone says or does something to offend you, you decide you have the right to teach them a lesson? Is that what happened with Cynthia? Did you teach her a lesson, Mary?"

CHAPTER 7

"*M*ary!" Paul pushed open the motel room door and burst inside. "Not another word, don't you say another word, understand me?"

"But Paul, I didn't do anything!" She could barely hold back the tears that burned in her eyes.

"You!" He turned on Kirk and pointed a finger right at him. "Out of here now."

"Excuse me?" Kirk narrowed his eyes. "I am in the middle of questioning a suspect."

"Are you going to arrest her?" Paul took another step towards him, his gray eyes unfaltering. "Are you?"

"Not at this time." Kirk gritted his teeth. "But that doesn't mean…"

"It means that you can leave." Paul crossed his

arms and gazed at him with such fury that even Mary was intimidated.

"We'll talk soon, Mary." Kirk tipped his hat to her, then stepped out of the motel room.

"Paul, now he'll think I'm angry at him." Mary groaned. "You shouldn't have done that."

"And you shouldn't be talking to a police officer without a lawyer," Paul said as Suzie stepped back into the room as well. "Mary, like it or not, as absurd as it may seem, you are a suspect, and you need to realize that."

"I didn't kill anyone." Mary sank down on the edge of the bed again. "I didn't."

"Of course, you didn't." Suzie sat down beside her and rubbed her hand along her knee. "No one thinks you did."

"Kirk does." She sniffled as tears slipped down her cheeks. "You should have seen the way he looked at me, Suzie. I'm sure that he was ready to put the handcuffs right on me. How could he think that about me? I've never been so mortified. Do I come across as a person that would murder someone?"

"He doesn't really think that, sweetie." Suzie took a deep breath. "He's just doing his job. Paul is right. You're a suspect, and there's no way we can deny that. I'm sure that Jason had Kirk question you because he knew that he could never ask you questions like that and it might be seen as a conflict of interest. I'm sorry, you did nothing to deserve that kind of treatment, but right now it's Kirk's job to try to get the truth, and that means asking a lot of uncomfortable questions. Boy, is Jason going to get an earful from me about the way Kirk acted. I could hear everything through the door. I'm sorry that he treated you that way. But it's time you get a lawyer."

"But I didn't do anything. So doesn't it make me look guilty if I hire a lawyer?"

"No." Paul sighed. "It makes you look smart. Like Wes told you, you need a lawyer to protect you. The facts of the case are pointing right in your direction, and no matter how many times you say you are innocent, unless you can prove that, you are still going to be their prime suspect. So please, hire a lawyer."

"Okay." She wiped away a few more tears that fell. "Yes, I guess I'd better."

"Good." Suzie wrapped her arm around her friend's shoulders. "I already have a few names we can look into."

"And until you have someone hired, do not speak to the police again. If they arrest you, you don't say a word until your lawyer gets to the station." Paul met her eyes. "That's very important, Mary."

"Arrest me?" She rubbed her wrist. "I can't even imagine being in handcuffs. How horrible."

"Hopefully it won't come to that." Paul offered a sympathetic frown.

"It won't." Suzie cut her gaze towards him. "We won't let it. We can't wait around for Jason and Kirk to get to the bottom of this. We need to figure out what happened for ourselves, no matter what it takes."

"I'm in," Paul said. "No matter what."

"I don't want you two to do anything that could get either of you into trouble." Mary wiped her eyes again. "I've caused enough trouble as it is."

"Mary, none of this is your fault," Suzie said. "You know that, don't you?"

"It is. If I had just gotten her breakfast right, if I hadn't interrupted her on set, then no one would have seen her upset with me, and the evidence wouldn't be pointing right at me. I should have done a better job."

"No sweetheart, you do an amazing job. What's happened here is a crime, and the only person responsible for any of it, is the monster that put poison in Cynthia's food. So, let's focus on that, all right?"

"Yes." Mary released a long shaky breath. "Yes, I can do that."

"Let's just assume that the food that you gave her was poisoned, Mary." Paul began to pace.

"What? No!" She shook her head. "It definitely wasn't."

"I know you didn't do it, but maybe someone decided to make it look like you did. Was there anyone hanging around the kitchen? Did anyone come in to taste test, or look through the cabinets?" He paused in front of her. "Anyone at all?"

"No." She thought for a moment, then pursed her lips. "No, no one. I'm careful about not leaving food out. I can't think of any time that someone might have slipped poison into the food. I'm sorry. I know that's not what you want to hear, but I honestly have no idea who could have done this."

"I have two ideas." Suzie crossed her arms. "Remember when we talked about Shawn? Well, I just thought about something that Marcus said when we found Cynthia. He said that they were going to work things out and get back together. That means there was some unrest in their marriage. I think it's possible that she rejected him, you heard the way that she spoke to him when he walked her to Dune House. She didn't want anything to do with him. Maybe she made it clear that their marriage was over, and he decided to kill her rather than lose her."

"Oh, that's possible." Mary frowned. "I hate to think it, but you're right. They certainly didn't act like a happy couple, did they?"

"That's something we can look into." Paul nodded. "I'm sure if they were unhappy other members of the crew knew about it. That sort of thing is hard to hide."

"Yes, Marcus is definitely a possibility. But I also found out some information from Ty about Shawn, and his history with Cynthia." Suzie nodded.

As they huddled together, she shared the story that Ty revealed to her.

"If he really lost so much, then I think he should be our main suspect," Suzie said.

"That may be, but how do we prove it?" Paul rubbed his hand along his chin. "Having motive isn't enough."

"No, it's not." Mary frowned. "And honestly, I don't think he did it. I know it sounds like he's a good suspect, but so do I, don't I?"

"Mary, you always see the best in people. I get

that, and I respect it, and admire it. But in this situation, we need to follow any lead we have, if it ends up not panning out, then that is fine. But it's still a lead." Suzie squeezed her hand. "Okay?"

"Okay." Mary sighed.

"I'll do some more research on Shawn and see if I can find out anything more about his connection with Cynthia. Paul, did you bring it?"

"Yes, I did, here." He reached into his bag and pulled out a laptop. "It's old, but it still works."

"Great, thank you so much."

"While you do that, I'm going to go get some breakfast." Mary picked up her purse and slipped out the door. As much as she appreciated her friends for helping her, she needed the chance to do some investigating of her own.

~

*M*ary didn't stop for breakfast in the lobby. By then it was crowded, and she had no interest in enduring the curious and judgmental looks that others would give her. Instead she walked towards Dune House. It was quite a long walk to get there from the motel, but she needed it. Even though the pain in her knees made it difficult for her to exercise, her body still craved it, and so did her mind. Whenever she had something to figure out, a good walk helped her get through it. However, she only made it about halfway before she knew she had to stop and rest. Luckily, she was right in front of the diner. She stepped inside to a small crowd, and found an empty spot at the counter. As she eased her way up on to the bar stool, a waitress walked up to her with a smile.

"Hi Mary. What can I get for you?"

"Coffee and toast, please." She offered a small smile. Did she know? Did she suspect her? It was hard to tell, as the waitress always had a sunny disposition. As she began to relax, she heard a familiar voice from behind her.

"Mary. How are you?" Marcus sat down on the stool beside her.

"Marcus, what are you doing here? They're giving away breakfast at the motel." She looked him over from head to toe. He still wore the same clothes he had on the night before. His hair was ruffled, and he clearly hadn't shaved.

"Yes, breakfast and aggravation. I couldn't risk running into Shawn or Ty again. I'm sorry that you saw that last night. I'm not usually like that, I swear." He frowned as he looked over at her. "Are you okay?"

"Yes. I should be the one asking you that." She looked into his eyes. "I'm so sorry."

"I'm still trying to process it all." He closed his eyes for a moment, then opened them again. "I just want you to know, I don't think you had anything to do with this."

"You don't?" She took a sharp breath. "Oh, you have no idea how good it is to hear that. I didn't, Marcus, I really didn't."

"I know." He smiled slightly. "When the police told me that you were their main suspect I laughed in their faces. You're a kind person, and never even said a cross word to Cynthia. Why would you want to kill her?" He shook his head. "I told the police exactly who to look at. Shawn. But for some reason they are dragging their feet on that."

"So you really think Shawn is capable of that?"

"Sure, why not? He's capable of a lot of things." His jaw trembled. It relaxed, when the waitress brought them both their food.

"If you need anything else, just let me know." She winked, then turned and walked away.

"Do you have any proof, any evidence that he

might have been involved?" Mary leaned closer to him.

"Don't you think if I did he'd be in handcuffs already?" He gazed at her for a moment. "Just because my wife and I fought, that doesn't mean that I didn't love her. I loved her so much that I was willing to forgive anything. We would have made things work. But now we'll never have that chance. He took that from us, and I am going to make sure that he pays for that."

"Slow down, slow down." She rested her hand on his arm. "It'll do no good to get yourself thrown in jail, will it? You need to keep your wits about you."

"How can I?" He sighed and stared down at his coffee. "I just don't know what to do. I used to do everything I could to protect her. But it's too late for that now. There is no way to protect her. I can't ever get her back." His eyes filled with tears. "I just keep seeing her there, at the bottom of the stairs."

"Oh Marcus." She slipped her arm around his shoulders. "I'm so sorry. This kind of loss, there's no way to explain it, or make it better."

"There's one way." He shrugged off her touch and met her eyes. "If Shawn is behind bars, it'll make it just a little easier."

"Well, anything you can think of to help with that, just tell the police. They will work hard to make sure that the killer is caught." She picked up her mug of coffee.

"Are you sure about that? Because right now, all I see is them trying to come after you." His tone was harsh as he studied her. "Maybe they're more interested in creating a local scandal than they are in the truth."

"No, that's not the case. I can assure you. They are very good at what they do." She set her coffee back down without taking a sip. "The truth will come out, Marcus."

"If you say so." He turned back to his coffee.

Mary realized she'd lost her appetite again. She left the cash for her and Marcus' breakfast, then excused herself. He didn't seem like a murderous husband, but then, she guessed if he did kill Cynthia, he would be doing his best to cover it up. As she stepped outside onto the sidewalk, she noticed a familiar face at the end of the street. She raised her hand to wave to Wes as he looked in her direction. However, he didn't wave back. He looked right past her, then turned and walked in the other direction. It felt like a slap in the face. It was possible he just didn't see her, but she doubted it.

Her stomach churned as she wondered if perhaps Wes was doing more than just his job. Maybe he was trying to send a message, that he was finished with their relationship. The thought bounced around her mind as she walked back towards the motel.

CHAPTER 8

*S*uzie looked up when the motel room door opened, and Mary stepped inside.

"Hi, how was your breakfast?"

"Uh, it was fine. I ran into Marcus." She dropped down on to the end of the bed beside her. "Where's Paul?"

"He went to run some errands for me. What did Marcus have to say?" She searched Mary's expression. She was certain that something was wrong, but there was so much going on that she wasn't sure if it was something new.

"He seems pretty convinced that Shawn did it."

"Well, he's not alone. I did some more research on Shawn." She turned the computer so that Mary could see it. "As it turns out, Cynthia did more than just ruin his future and reputation, she apparently also broke his heart."

"What?" Mary skimmed over the information on the screen. "Who wrote this?"

"Shawn did. He posted it on social media, and deleted it, but not before a few people reposted it, eventually it ended up being reposted a bunch of times. From the sound of it, she had been having an affair with him."

"Was she married to Marcus at the time?" Mary finished reading the words and shivered a little. "Wow, he was ruthless in his description of her. It's hard to believe that he ever had any feelings for her when he uses that kind of language against her."

"Yes, well in his eyes she did essentially ruin his life. And yes, she was married to Marcus. She's been married to him for ten years, high school sweethearts and then they married not long after college."

"Do you think it's possible that Shawn was lying about their affair?" Mary took the computer into her lap. "Maybe he was so angry about what happened that he wanted to cause her harm by trying to disrupt her marriage?"

"It's possible. But it didn't work, since she and Marcus are still married." Suzie frowned.

"Maybe that's why he said what he did, about

working things out. Maybe he and Cynthia were still trying to work through the affair, or the supposed affair, between her and Shawn. He said to me today that Shawn was capable of a lot of things, and that he was willing to forgive Cynthia for anything. Even an affair?"

"If so, that's quite a long time to be working on things. It's been close to three years since all of this took place. But their history certainly gives Shawn plenty of motive to kill Cynthia."

"But why now?" Mary handed the computer back. "Why would he wait so long to take his revenge?"

"From what I overheard on that phone call, he was livid that she'd been allowed to be part of the crew that he was on. It seems to me that he's been doing his best to avoid her personally and professionally, so perhaps when he was forced to work with her again, everything just came to the surface, and he decided he couldn't take it anymore."

"Yes, it's possible." Mary frowned.

"With his knowledge about chemicals and toxins from his documentary, I'm guessing he could figure out what he could poison her food with. Once Summer is able to isolate the poison, I'm sure all of this will be settled." Suzie placed her hand over Mary's. "It's just a matter of time now."

"Yes." She smiled as she looked over at Suzie. "I'm sure you are right about that."

"Why don't we go out? I just got a text from Paul, he's back at the boat. It would be good to get some fresh air." Suzie stood up and pulled her friend to her feet as well.

"I don't know." Mary glanced towards the window. "I'm sure everyone in town is talking about me being a suspect. I'm not sure that I feel like facing all of that. Even when I was at the diner, I had a hard time. I can't stop imagining what other people must be thinking about me."

"It's all the more reason to face it, Mary. Don't hide away, when you have nothing to be ashamed of, there's no reason to do that. Besides, when all of this is over, we're still going to be living in the same little town, and the people here need to know that you had nothing to do with this."

"All right, all right." She grabbed her shawl from the dresser and brushed her long auburn hair aside as she put it on. "Some fresh air would be good, and I want to see if Paul has heard anything new. You know how those fishermen like to talk."

"Such gossips." Suzie laughed as she opened the

door and they stepped outside.

Mary smiled, but no laughter escaped her. Suzie caught sight of a flicker of pain in her eyes.

"Mary." She paused as they reached the parking lot. "There's something else going on, isn't there?"

"It's nothing." She forced a smile.

"No, it's not. You can tell me, hon, you know that." She took her hand and gave it a squeeze. "No matter what it is."

"Oh Suzie, you know me too well." She sighed and leaned up against the car. "I saw Wes."

"You did?" Suzie smiled. "Did he have anything to say about the case? Is he doing okay?"

"I have no idea." She lowered her eyes. "I waved to him, but it was like he didn't even see me, and then he turned and walked away. I didn't even speak to him. He didn't acknowledge me at all." She looked back up at her friend. "I have a feeling that this case is going to be the end of things for us."

"Oh, Mary don't say that. Maybe things weren't what they seemed. Maybe he really didn't see you. I don't think that Wes would treat you that way." She frowned, then narrowed her eyes. "And if he did, I'll make sure he never does again."

"Just relax, Suzie it's okay. I mean, it's not like I thought things would last forever. Let's just go. It's not that important, I don't want to talk about it anymore." She pulled open the passenger side door.

As Suzie walked around to the other side of the car she tried to think of something comforting or supportive to say, but she was too preoccupied by exactly what she would say to Wes the next time she saw him. Mary was her best friend and as close as a sister to her, but she was more than that. She was a good person who had gone through bad times in her life. She didn't need to endure any more hurt.

~

Suzie and Mary drove together to the harbor. With Dune House in sight, it was hard for Suzie to hold back her emotion. It had only been a short time since she was there, and yet it seemed like an eternity. She hated to think of what the crime scene investigation team had done to the inside of the house. She'd seen what happened on television shows, where every drawer was emptied, every closet torn apart. She guessed they would have a lot of cleaning up to do when they were finally able to return to Dune House.

Paul met them at the entrance of the boat and welcomed them inside.

"I'm glad that you're here. I just found out some information about the case."

"From who?" Suzie asked.

"Jason."

"Why did he tell you instead of me?"

"I think because I happened to speak to him shortly after he had found out the information. I'm sure he'll share it with you soon."

"What did Jason have to say? What did they find?" Suzie asked.

"It's more about what they didn't find. According to what Jason told me, no poisoned food or drink was found in Cynthia's room at the motel or in her belongings." He frowned. "Presuming it was food that was poisoned, that leads to one particular question. If we know, which we do, that nothing in Dune House contained the poison, then what food was poisoned? Mary, you said you provided all of the food for breakfast, and for lunch on set. Right?"

"Yes, I did. And no, none of it was poisoned. I am so careful with the food, as I would never want someone's vacation to be ruined by a case of food poisoning or even just a food allergy. I do my best to make sure there is no cross contamination, and I clean constantly. I really do try."

"We know." Suzie met her eyes with a reassuring smile. "No one doubts that."

"I'm sorry." She took a deep breath. "I'm just so sensitive at this point."

"That's all right, Mary. Just know I'm not questioning you, all right?" Paul looked into her eyes. "I'm only trying to help."

"Thanks Paul." Mary managed a small smile.

"Now, if none of the food you provided was poisoned that means that Cynthia must have gotten food from somewhere else, right? So, did you notice anything on the refreshments table near the set? Did you hear about someone offering her food? Did anyone bring in food to breakfast?"

"No. Not that I noticed." She closed her eyes for a moment and thought about the refreshment table. "No, I'm certain there was nothing else on the table. Besides, the entire cast and crew were filming all morning, I'm not sure that any of them would have had time to go and pick anything else up."

"Summer relayed to Jason that the poison was fast acting. It would have killed her within two hours maximum. So, it had to be something that she ingested around lunch time. Mary, you saw her about one o'clock, going to Drake's room, right?"

"Yes. And then, when we found her, it was close to two."

"If her upset stomach was from the poison, then that means we only have about an hour window of when she could have eaten whatever was poisoned." He scratched his hand back through his hair and frowned. "It seems like it would be so simple to solve."

"But, as far as we know she was on set for that entire window." Suzie crossed her arms and began to pace. "So, that narrows down our suspects. The set is roped off, there is security, they're not going to let some random person on set."

"Yes, but Cynthia was part of the crew. She could have wandered off set, but not for long." Mary settled into a chair. "However, that still limits our suspects. If it was Shawn, he would have been on set, so it would have been impossible for him to disappear, lace food, and plant it somewhere that Cynthia would eat it, with no one noticing him going missing, or seeing him tampering with the food."

"I wouldn't say impossible." Suzie tapped her chin. "But very difficult."

"Yes, I'll agree to that. I suppose he could have slipped something into the food on the refreshments table when no one was looking, but remember, I gave Cynthia's food directly to her. Unless she handed it off to someone, which certainly wouldn't have been Shawn, it couldn't have been tampered with."

"Hmm, if they couldn't leave the set to pick anything up, and they couldn't have gotten to her food to spike it, then maybe someone had something delivered?" Suzie looked between the two. "It's possible that one of the local restaurants or shops delivered to the set. People will do just about anything for a celebrity."

"Yes, you're right." Mary snapped her fingers. "That could have happened. But are you saying you think that someone that lives and works around here would have poisoned the food? If they poisoned a large amount, why did only Cynthia fall ill?"

"No, I don't think that. Cynthia was targeted, and I doubt that she knew anyone around here well enough for them to be so filled with hate that they would want to murder her. But I do think that perhaps someone on set ordered food, and then poisoned that food, before it was given to Cynthia. Considering her dietary requirements maybe she had a special meal delivered, or everyone could have been eating the same thing and the murderer may have made sure that Cynthia got the poisoned portion."

"Yes, that makes sense." Paul nodded. "We can check into that easily enough. Most places will keep records of their deliveries, tomorrow morning we can check with all of the shops and restaurants to see if anyone delivered to the set yesterday."

"Good idea." Suzie smiled. "Now, I feel like we have a direction we can go in."

"Yes, thank you, Paul." Mary forced a brighter smile. "I can't thank you enough for your help."

"Mary, you don't have to thank me. We're friends, and I will always do whatever I can to back you up."

"And the same goes for you, Paul." She stood up. "I think I'm going to step outside for a few minutes."

"I'll come with you." Suzie followed after her out of the boat.

~

Mary walked along the harbor, with Suzie at her side, and her mind in turmoil. She appreciated her friend's presence, but she also knew that she expected an explanation for her mood.

"I'm sorry, Suzie, I know I should be focused on Cynthia's murder, but I just keep thinking about Wes walking away from me today." Mary frowned. "Do you think he suspects that I did this?"

"Of course not, Mary. He could never. I think he either didn't see you, or he was distracted by the case."

Mary paused beside the railing that lined the water.

"I know it's unreasonable of me to expect him to help me. But I'm in real trouble now. If I get arrested, the kids will find out, and what will I tell them? How will I explain it to them?" She pulled the shawl tighter around her shoulders and gazed out across the harbor. "I thought Wes would be a little more supportive I suppose."

"I understand that. I honestly wish he'd be more helpful, too. But he's also restricted by his badge. It's not easy to carry it. You've seen how Jason has had to struggle between helping us and remaining loyal to his role as a police officer. It's very difficult for him." She gazed at her friend's face, and could see the hurt there. It was hard for her not to want to march right up to Wes and knock him on the nose.

Mary had always been such a loyal and dedicated friend, she would do anything to protect someone who was in trouble, no matter what risk it caused her.

"Look at Paul." Mary glanced over at her. "He will literally do anything to protect you. He would go out into a stormy ocean in a life raft to keep you safe. He would walk the edge of legal and illegal in a heartbeat if it meant it would help you." She took a deep breath and then released her words along with a sigh. "I really think that he suspects me."

"You really think that?" Suzie's eyes widened. "Wes would never believe that you are capable of something like this."

"No? Then why isn't he protecting me?" She frowned. "It might be because, just like Kirk said, he has to follow the facts. The facts point to me, and perhaps Wes doubts whether I'm telling the truth when I say that I'm innocent. As you said, he's a police officer, and that badge can be quite a burden to carry. Maybe he doesn't want to be associated with a criminal, with someone accused of something so terrible."

"First of all, you haven't been accused of anything. You haven't been arrested, and you're not going to be. Second of all, if Wes is enough of a fool to suspect something like that about you, then he's not worth your time. He obviously doesn't know a thing about you if he could even for a second imagine that you could be involved in this."

"I know, I know." She closed her eyes. "Maybe that's the most hurtful part. Perhaps I thought there was more between us than there really was. I guess I got a little caught up in the idea of a new love, when really, I should have learned my lesson the first time."

"Just give it a little time, Mary. All of this is going to be cleared up soon. Hmm?" She searched her friend's eyes. "I know there is so much on your mind right now, but the important thing is that you don't lose faith. All of this is going to be in the past sooner than you think."

"I sure hope so." Mary shifted back towards the railing and studied the darkened sky over the still sea. "Because I'm not sure how much more I can take." She shuddered as she tightened the shawl around her. It seemed fitting that a storm would brew as her emotions wreaked havoc on her mind.

"What about Preston?"

"Hmm?" Mary blinked and looked over at Suzie. "What about him?"

"What if he had something to do with this?

Maybe the only reason he let Cynthia work on the set was to give him the opportunity to kill her." Suzie gazed down into the murky water near the edge of the walkway. "He's the one that authorized her being on set after all."

"Yes, he did, but why would Preston want to kill her?"

"I'm not sure." She pursed her lips. "But as the director he must know as much if not more about what is happening behind the scenes than anyone else. I'm willing to bet, even if he didn't kill Cynthia, he has a good idea who did. I think I should talk to him."

"Good luck finding him though. He wasn't even staying at Dune House or the motel. He had his own private suite in Parish." Mary shook her head. "He seems a bit elitist."

"Someone must know where he is though." She thought about it for a second. "Maybe Ty? They would have to be in contact, wouldn't they?"

"I would think so. I have his number. I could check with him." Mary pulled out her phone. "He wanted me to be able to reach him."

"That's nice of him." She rested her elbow on the railing and waited while Mary called.

"Hi Ty, it's Mary. Oh yes, I'm fine thank you.

Do you happen to know where Preston might be staying?" She glanced over at Suzie. "He's there now?" A frown crossed her lips. "All right. That's okay. Oh wait, really?" She gave Suzie a thumbs up. "Thanks so much, Ty."

"What is it?" Suzie stepped closer as Mary hung up the phone.

"He told me the hotel he's staying at, but apparently right now he's out to lunch. He invited Ty to join him but he declined. He's at Andover's."

"Wow, that's a bit of a dive for a man like him." Suzie raised an eyebrow. "I think I'll go see if he still wants company."

"I'll come with you." Mary tucked her phone back into her purse.

"No, Mary. I want you well rested for whatever comes next. Besides, it's possible that he will clam up around you, since he knows..." Her voice trailed off.

"That I'm a suspect." Mary sighed. "You're right. Can you drop me off at the library though? I want to check in with Louis about a few things."

"Sure, I will. That's a good idea."

CHAPTER 9

*A*fter Suzie dropped Mary off at the library, she headed for Andover's. It was a nice enough restaurant, but it wasn't the type of place she would expect a wealthy director to dine. Though, to be fair there weren't a lot of five star restaurants in Parish or Garber. When she stepped inside she noticed Preston right away. He was hard to miss as he was seated alone at a six-person table and all of the tables around him were empty, while others were packed in pretty tight. She guessed that he'd asked for some space between him and the other diners. She wondered if he'd be willing to let her sit down. After a deep breath and some built up determination she walked over to the table.

"Hi Preston. How are you this evening?"

"Hmm?" He looked up from his phone with a dazed expression. "Who are you?"

"Suzie, I run Dune House with my business partner, Mary." She studied him for a long moment. They'd had at least five conversations, was it really possible that he had no idea who she was?

"Oh right. And?"

"Do you mind if I sit?" She rested her hand on the back of one of the extra chairs.

"Oh, my food is on its way." He caught sight of the waitress as she carried a tray towards them. "I guess, just for a minute."

"Okay, thanks." She settled in the chair and did her best to hold her tongue. He certainly wasn't the most polite man she'd ever met.

The waitress set the pasta down in front of him, then pulled out her order pad.

"What would you like, ma'am?" She smiled.

"No, she's not eating." He picked up his fork and looked at his plate. "Hm."

"Is something wrong?" The waitress leaned closer.

"It's fine." He set his fork down.

"Preston, have a bite," the waitress said.

He gazed at the food on his plate, then looked up at the waitress who stood beside him.

"Why are you so interested in me eating?"

"I'm sorry, I'm just such a big fan, and I'd love to know what you think of the meal." She clasped her hands together in front of her and offered him a sweet smile.

"Uh huh. I'm hesitant to eat anything in this town." He pushed his food around on his plate. "Who knows what could be in it."

"I promise, there's nothing wrong with it. Would you like me to take a bite?" She picked up a fork from the extra settings on the table.

"Yes, actually, I would." He watched as she scooped up a forkful of his food and placed it into her mouth. As she chewed, she smiled, and offered a soft moan of approval. "It's really good."

"We shall see." He took a bite himself. A second later he nodded. "Not bad, not bad at all. Now, what did you say you wanted?" He looked across the table at Suzie.

"I just wanted to check in with you. I know all of this has to be so frustrating for you."

"Frustrating?" He stared across the table at her. "Is that really the word you think I should use?" He chuckled. "Or maybe you just want to hear me be full of myself and say that my work should come before the death of some insignificant person?"

"I wouldn't expect you to say that." She cleared her throat, and tried to ignore the fact that he was absolutely right about her opinion of him.

"Sure you would, so would everyone. Do you know that even Ty expected that I would insist on continuing to film? Like I'm some kind of beast." He shook his head and took another bite of his food. "No, a woman died. Her death needs to be settled the best it can before we begin filming again. I had a friend who pushed through the death of a crew member to get his show ready on time. The stories I heard about the so-called accidents on that set were horrifying. No way, I'm not letting anyone's angry spirit derail my plans for this show to be a blockbuster hit."

"Ah." She blinked, then stared a bit more closely at him. Was he joking? From the furrow of his brow and his lack of laughter she could only assume that he wasn't. "I suppose that is as good a reason as any."

"Sure it is." He looked up at her. "You know, I argued with Ty about bringing her on. He insisted, and I said, Ty, she's trouble. Every set she's ever worked on, there have been problems. She got herself quite a reputation after that incident with Shawn's film, you know. It was ridiculous that he asked me. But what Ty wants, Ty gets."

"Really? I didn't realize that actors had that much power and influence on a production."

"Ty does. He's already a household name, and if he doesn't put his all in, then my show will stink, and it won't stand a chance. The one good thing Cynthia brought to my show though, was the location."

"The location? You mean here in Garber?" Suzie leaned forward some.

"Yes, she suggested it. I guess she grew up around here somewhere. Anyway, we needed a location on a beach that matched the setting in the script. We needed to keep the location as private as possible and have exclusive use of it so we could film the pilot. It's impossible to book in places like Florida and California, never mind the islands, so when she suggested this place I jumped on it. It fitted our limited budget. I'm surprised more people haven't used it. It's not a big beach, but it does just fine for what we need, and so far the town has been quite accommodating." He paused with his fork halfway to his mouth. "Aside from the murder of course."

"I didn't realize that Cynthia grew up around here. Did she ever mention where?"

"No." He shrugged and finished his bite of food. "I didn't care to ask either. I bet she wishes she'd never had a homecoming now though."

"So, you think it was a local person that committed this crime?"

"Sure, why not? Maybe she went off and lived her dream, and someone back home didn't like that. Maybe she upset someone. I don't know. I doubt it would be anyone on my crew. I mean, why would they risk it?"

"Sometimes people just get angry. I've heard that you were pretty angry with Cynthia on the day she died."

"Angry?" He laughed. "My natural state is angry, honey. When I'm on set, my nerves are on edge. Everything has to be perfect, then one idiot makes one stupid mistake, and we all have to start all over again. Wouldn't that make you angry?"

"Yes, it probably would."

"Then you can understand why I was angry with Cynthia. She brought in someone who was unprofessional. That's basically like spitting in my face."

"I'm sure it set your timeline behind. That must have been very frustrating."

"Not as frustrating as having to halt my entire production for a murder investigation." He pointed his fork at her. "So, before you try to accuse me of anything, consider what Cynthia's death is costing me. It wouldn't make any sense for me to cause her any harm, would it?"

"No, I suppose not."

"No, you suppose not." He laughed again and pushed his food around on his plate. "Well maybe this isn't poisoned, but it certainly isn't food either." He snapped at the waitress. "Hey! This is disgusting! I'm not paying you a dime."

Suzie rolled her eyes as she stood up from the table. She decided not to point out that he'd complimented the waitress on the taste shortly before and eaten almost the entire plate before he complained. What would be the point? She fired off a quick text to Mary with the information she had just learned as she walked towards the door. When she left the restaurant, the waitress was in tears. She was tempted to tell Preston exactly what she thought of him, but she didn't want to alienate him, not just yet. After all, he'd just given them a new lead, one she never would have even considered. Did Cynthia used to live in the area? Could there be someone local involved in the murder?

~

*M*ary was relieved to see that the library was mostly empty. Although she'd wanted to be brave and face the rest of the town, she wasn't sure that she had the backbone for it. Luckily Louis greeted her with open arms.

"Mary! It's good to see you. I'm sorry all of this happened under your roof. If there's anything I can do to help just let me know."

"Actually, that's why I'm here." She smiled some as she returned his hug. She could always count on Louis to be friendly, although he was quite harsh to others, especially those that spoke too loudly in the library. "I was wondering if there's a way to look into someone's background, more than just social media. I mean, to look into places they've lived, and worked. That kind of thing."

"Who are we investigating?" He quirked an eyebrow.

"Cynthia. I just feel like I want to know more about her. I didn't have the chance to get to know her very well. Is that possible?" She glanced over his shoulder at his computer.

"Sure. There's a way we can look into that."

Louis settled in a chair in front of one of the computers and pushed his glasses up along his nose. He began typing, then paused. "Do you know her maiden name?"

"No, I don't." She frowned.

"All right, let's take a look and see if we can find the information."

As he began typing, Mary's cell phone buzzed with a text. She blushed.

"Sorry, I'll turn the sound off."

"Please do." Louis cleared his throat.

Before she turned the volume down she noticed the message was from Suzie. Her eyes widened when she read it.

"Louis, can you change that search? It turns out that Cynthia may have lived around here at some point. Can you narrow down the search to figure out where?"

"Sure, I can. I just found her maiden name. It's French." His eyes widened. "I know that a French family lived in Parish, but I don't know much about them, maybe she's a part of that family."

"Maybe."

"Cynthia French, did you have an address around here at some point?" After a few minutes, he pointed to the screen. "Here she is as a high school graduate from Parish High."

"Oh wow, Louis, you are amazing." Mary smiled as she peered over his shoulder at the screen. "Is there a home address?"

"Yes, I'll get it for you." He jotted it down on a slip of paper and handed it to her. "I can't tell you if she's related to the people that currently live there, and I'm not sure how much it will help, but I hope it does."

"Thank you so much, Louis." She grasped the paper tightly. In that second it seemed as if it was the first promising lead that might unravel the truth about Cynthia's death.

"You're welcome, Mary." He caught her hand and held it for a moment. "I just want you to know that I never thought you were involved in any of this, not for a second. Okay?"

"Yes." She sighed with relief. "Thank you, it means a lot to me to hear that."

"Tell Suzie I say hello, and I am well aware that she has not returned that overdue library book yet." He straightened his tie. "Those fines add up you know."

"Oops, yes I will tell her. I'm sure she will get it back in right away."

"See that she does." He swiveled on his chair back to his computer.

She tucked the address into her pocket and hurried out of the library. Just as she stepped outside, Suzie pulled into the parking lot.

"Mary, I'm so glad I caught you." She pulled up close to the curb.

"Me too." Mary settled into the passenger seat. "When you texted me that Cynthia lived somewhere nearby at one time, I asked Louis how to find her previous address, and he found it for me." She presented the slip of paper. "It's possible that someone she knows still lives there, or nearby."

"Yes, you're right." She typed the address into her GPS. "We should check it out. I had such an interesting conversation with Preston. I don't think we can rule him out as a suspect."

"Really? It seems like a huge risk for him to take."

"Sometimes people get so full of themselves that they truly believe they can get away with anything, including murder. It's possible that he just lost his temper."

"But losing your temper doesn't usually lead to murder by poisoning someone. That's more of a pre-meditated situation."

"Yes, you're right about that. However, I still think he's a possible suspect. Just the way he spoke about her turned my stomach. Then of course, there's always Marcus."

"Yes, Marcus. He had the opportunity and motive, too."

"You know I was thinking, there's this philosophy of once a cheater always a cheater. What if she started a relationship with someone new?" Suzie glanced over at her. "If Marcus found out, it would have killed him."

"That's true. I'm not sure that I agree with that theory. But it could have happened. She did seem pretty close to the actor she was defending on the set when I brought her lunch. Maybe it was him?"

"Maybe. There's only one way to find out. But first, let's see where this address leads us."

CHAPTER 10

The GPS led Suzie and Mary into Parish. It was a fine town, a bit bigger than Garber, with a much busier beach that attracted many more tourists due to its size. It was without the quaintness of little shops and perfectly manicured lawns. It was a mixture of urban and small town, with tall shiny buildings, and neglected old block houses. It boasted a much larger police department, of which Wes was one of the finest detectives. Thinking of him, reminded Suzie of how he treated Mary. It worried her, too, as she wondered if he knew more than he was willing to say. Was it possible that there was so much evidence against Mary that an arrest was inevitable?

"Are you sure this is the right address?" Suzie

glanced over at Mary as she pulled to a stop in front of the location that the GPS identified.

"Yes, that's the address that Louis gave me. But he did say he had no idea who lived there now." She scanned the overgrown front yard and boarded up windows.

"I don't think anyone does, and probably no one has for quite some time." Suzie pushed the car into park, and frowned. "I guess this was a wasted trip."

"Not necessarily." Mary pointed towards the houses on either side of the abandoned home. "The neighbors might know something about Cynthia. Should we ask?"

"That driveway has a car in it. Let's check it out." Suzie stepped out of the car, and Mary followed behind her. When Suzie knocked on the door, a stout young woman answered within seconds.

"Yes? Can I help you?" She had a bright smile on her face.

"Hello, we have some questions about the property next door."

"Oh, I was so hoping that you were from code enforcement. Finally, all of my complaints are paying off!" She pushed open the screen door. "Come inside, I can tell you everything."

"I'm sorry for the confusion, but we're not from code enforcement. We're here trying to track down information about a woman named Cynthia French. Did you know her?" She searched her eyes with fading hope. She looked too young to have lived in the house for too long.

"Oh, you aren't code enforcement." Her smile slumped. "You have no idea how frustrating it's been for me. I call, and call, and no one comes out to do anything about this property. It's horrible. The bugs in the summer are the worst, and then of course the neighborhood kids think it's a good place to hide out and do their drugs. It's just a hazard!" She still stepped aside to allow them inside. "Cynthia?" She walked over to her couch and sat down. "What do you want to know about her?"

"Did you know her?" Suzie sat down in an armchair, while Mary perched on the other side of the couch.

"Sure. We grew up next door to each other. At one point we were friends. Of course, that all changed when she became too good for everyone in Parish." She rolled her eyes. "I guess karma really does bite you eventually, huh? All of her fancy connections don't mean anything in the great beyond, do they?"

"So, you've heard?" Suzie narrowed her eyes some. "It must have been quite a shock to hear that your childhood friend was murdered."

"Not really. She had that kind of personality that rubbed people up the wrong way. I'm amazed she made it out of Parish without more scars and stitches than she had. She was always getting into fights at school."

"Fights? About what?" Mary turned on the couch some to face her.

"She had this idea in her head that she was going to be a star. Now, here's the thing about that, she came from one of the poorest families in Parish. That's why the house is the way it is. Cynthia's family lost the place to foreclosure years ago. They kept saying she was going to help them out, but I guess the check never came. The padlock did, and it's been sitting like that empty ever since." She rolled her eyes. "So, the whole neighborhood has to pay the price. Anyway, she never shut up about being this big star, and making it rich. It irked people and they would pick at her about it. When Cynthia had enough she would blow up and attack them. Tempers run in that family."

"You must have known them pretty well." Mary

rested her hands in her lap. "Do you know where Cynthia's parents went?"

"They took the boy and moved away. I have no idea where. One evening they were there, the next morning they were gone. It was a little creepy to be honest. I would have called the cops if it weren't for the cops and bank showing up the next day with the padlocks. I guess they decided to just leave everything behind." She shrugged.

"You mentioned a boy, was that Cynthia's brother?" Suzie scooted forward in the chair. "I didn't realize she had a sibling."

"Yes, he was a few years younger than her, not quite eighteen when they lost the house. Ryan." She nodded. "His name was Ryan. A nice kid, shy. Not like the rest of them."

"Ryan?" Mary repeated the name as her eyes widened. "Are you sure that's his name?"

"Yes, like I said, he was a nice kid. As far as I know when they lost the house, he had to leave school and his friends. I always thought it was really sad for him. They kept saying that Cynthia was going to pull through and take care of the late payments, but she never did." She shook her head. "Now, I'm left to deal with the eyesore."

"That must be very frustrating." Suzie cleared

her throat. "Is there anything else you can tell us about Cynthia? Did she have a boyfriend?"

"No, not just one, anyway. She dated around. She always went for the bad boys, and then she would cheat on them, and the boys would beat each other up over her. It was pathetic really. She always gloated about how she could get them to fight. Honestly, she just became this terrible person." She glanced at her watch. "I have to go. I'm working a late shift tonight. Good luck with your search, ladies."

She walked them to the door.

As soon as they were back in the car, Suzie looked over at Mary. "Ryan is her…"

"Brother!" Mary finished for her.

"It's possible that it's a coincidence. They have different last names."

"Yes, but maybe he changed it if he wanted to get into acting, or they had different fathers."

"Ryan is a very common name." Suzie tucked her lip under her teeth and gnawed for a moment. "But, what are the chances?"

"We know that Cynthia insisted on Ryan being hired. She basically risked her job for it. So maybe she was trying to look out for her kid brother?"

"Hm. Think about it, Mary. If she really did

abandon her family, cause them to lose their house, and be ridiculed by their neighbors, maybe Ryan was looking for revenge?"

"Against his own sister?" She cringed. "I hate to think that's a possibility, but you're right, it very well could be. I think it's time we had a conversation with Ryan."

"Absolutely, the only question is, will he be willing to talk to us?" Suzie turned down the road that led back to Garber. "I hope that we can figure out what really happened to Cynthia. If Ryan is her brother, and he didn't do this, I can't imagine the pain that he's going through."

"I think he'd be willing to talk to me. It's getting a bit late now. Maybe I should go on my own tomorrow morning." She glanced at Suzie. "Is that okay?"

"Sure, it is. But if you need backup, you know I'll be there." She smiled.

"Thanks Suzie."

~

*A*fter breakfast the next morning Mary headed straight out in search of Ryan. It didn't take her long to find him. She strolled along the harbor, then down into the small park that bordered both the harbor and some open span of beach. It was a popular place for tourists, and she noticed him perched on one of the benches closest to the entrance.

"Hi Ryan." Mary sat down on the bench beside him.

"Hi." He shifted his feet against the grass then glanced over at her. "Mary, right?"

"Yes. How are you holding up?"

"Better than you." He scuffed his shoe across the ground. "I know that people think you did it."

"Some people might." She shrugged as she stared at her hands, which rested on her knees. "But I didn't."

"I didn't think you did." He wiped at his brow. "You don't seem the type to do something like that."

"Thanks." She scooted a little closer to him on the bench. "You and Cynthia were friends, weren't you?"

"You could say that. She helped me out."

"How did you two meet?"

"At a casting call. I was there, and she was there as a support person. She was going to help pick out those that would be selected to move on to the next stage. I didn't make it, but she gave me her card and told me she knew of the perfect acting job for me. Something to get my foot in the door that would probably lead to some bigger acting jobs."

"This one?" Mary glanced past him at the people that walked along the street.

"Yes. She said she'd make sure I got in."

"Did she ever tell you why?"

"She said she knew what it was like to start out, and that I needed some polishing, but that I had what it took to really make it. I didn't know whether to believe her or not. But it turned out she was right, she got me the role, and I messed it up, like always." He rolled his eyes.

"What makes you think that?" She studied him closely.

"You heard the way Preston yelled at me. You were there. He wishes I was never part of the show." His cheeks flushed.

"I think he's just a temperamental person. He probably didn't mean it."

"He meant it." He took a deep breath. "And he's right. I wasn't ready for this. I thought it was what I wanted, but it was just too much too fast. I was going to quit, but Cynthia told me that she would look like a fool if I did. She insisted I stick it out. So

I tried." He rubbed his hand through his hair. "But it didn't get any better."

"And now, are you going to quit?"

"I don't know." He looked over at her. "I should, shouldn't I? But, a part of me feels like I still owe her. Maybe I owe her even more now that she's gone."

"It would be a nice way to honor her memory I think, if you stuck it out. But you have to do what's right for you."

"Yes, I'll think about it."

"I guess you spent a good amount of time with her, working on things." She met his eyes. "Did she ever mention why she was so interested in you?"

"No, I don't think there was any special reason, she just wanted to help me. I felt like her project. I don't know, maybe she was trying to live her dreams through me or something. She told me that she wanted to be a star, but never had the look to be in front of a camera."

"Hmm, maybe that was the case. I'm sorry that you lost your sister, Ryan. And, for what it's worth, I'm sure Cynthia really knew her stuff. If she thought that you had that special something, then I bet you do."

He froze, at the word sister, just as she expected him to.

"What did you just say?" He looked over at her with wide eyes.

"I know she was your sister, Ryan." She placed her hand over his. "I know that you had a very hard life growing up, and that your parents lost their house. Is that when you went to Cynthia for help?"

"No." He rolled his eyes. "I would never do that. She came to me. It was like all of a sudden she grew a heart. She showed up one day at the place I was staying and said she would get me a job, get me into show business. I wasn't sure about it, but she insisted. I figured it couldn't hurt. But she told me that we had to keep our relationship a secret, or it might hurt my ability to get hired."

"I see. Was she always trying to help you when you were younger? Were you two close?" She listened attentively to every word he spoke.

"No, we weren't close. In fact, I spent most of my life believing that she hated me. It was hard not to think it, since she was always shouting it in my face." He narrowed his eyes.

"That sounds rough."

"It was. But it wasn't really her fault. Our parents were horrible. The only time they would speak to either of us, was to yell, or to make us fight. It was ugly, real ugly. When they lost the house, I thought they'd hunt her down. But they didn't. They just disappeared. I found a friend's couch to crash on, and tried to figure out what I would do next. Then out of the blue she showed up, too late for the house, but maybe that was because she didn't want to do anything that would help them."

"It's nice that the two of you patched things up."

"We didn't exactly." He peered over at her. "She got me this job, and everything, but it wasn't like all of a sudden she was all hugs and kind words. She still kept her distance. I thought maybe if I told her I forgave her for taking off the way she did, it would ease some of the tension, but instead she got angry. She went off on a rant about how she didn't owe our parents anything, and that I should learn to be independent like she was. I don't know, I think she expected me to be like her. But I'm not."

"You don't have to be, Ryan. It must have been hard for you to lose your home like that." She pursed her lips for a moment. "Were you ever angry at Cynthia for letting that happen?"

"No. Not really. My parents wanted people to think that she was some rich person, and that she planned to take care of them. But she never said she would do that. She didn't talk to them at all. They were not kind to either of us, but they were really hard on her. Maybe because she was the oldest." He looked down at his hands, then looked up at her again. "I was really just getting the chance to know her, and now she's gone."

"I'm sorry, Ryan. I can only imagine your grief. It's not going to be easy, but you will get through it."

"Thanks, Mary." He smiled at her as she stood up. "You're a very sweet person."

"Good luck." As Mary headed back towards the car, she thought about Cynthia. She'd heard plenty of stories about how terrible she was, but knowing she'd taken her younger brother under her wing, revealed a different side to her. She wasn't just demanding or cruel, she cared enough to steer Ryan in the right direction.

CHAPTER 11

*A*fter Suzie returned from breakfast she had just settled into the motel room to do some research when she heard a knock on the door. When she opened the door, she found a maid on the other side.

"Ma'am, would you like your room cleaned?" She smiled.

"No thanks, I can take care of it." Suzie smiled in return, then swung the door closed. She'd hoped it would be Jason, saying that it was time to go back home. The thought made her pull out her phone. She dialed his number, then began to pace. She knew he couldn't tell her much, if anything about the case, but she also needed to speak to him. She needed to feel connected, even if she truly wasn't. After two rings, he answered the phone.

"Hi Suzie. I'm sorry, I can't talk long."

"That's all right. Anything new on the case?"

"I can't tell you, you know that."

"What about an estimate of when we can get back into Dune House? That shouldn't be breaking any laws, I just want to know when I might be able to go back home. Is that so much to ask?" She took a breath to try to calm down. Despite the fact that she fully intended to be kind and patient with him, when she actually got on the phone, she found that her mouth raced to keep up with the pattern of her heartbeat.

"Okay, okay, slow down. I know this is difficult for you, but keep in mind, we have a victim in the middle of all of this."

"I do understand that, of course I do, but how long can it take to process the house? You have to be getting close to being done now."

"Nothing left unturned." He cleared his throat. "That's the only way to solve a crime like this."

"Jason, you have to give me something here. It's been two days. When do you think we can be back in Dune House?" She pressed the phone against her ear so that she wouldn't miss a single thing he said.

"I know you're frustrated, but there's not much I

can tell you. It's a large place with a lot of contents and that takes time."

"Look, I don't want to interfere in the investigation, you know that, but it's just making me so uneasy to be away from there. And to think of police officers rifling through my underwear drawer."

"Yes, I can see why that would make you uneasy." He chuckled.

"It's not funny, Jason! How about if I go to your house and dump out all of your drawers?" She took a deep breath to calm herself down. "I'm sorry."

"No, you're right. It's not funny. I know it's uncomfortable. I can tell you that the only reason it's taking this long is because of what we haven't found. There's no evidence of any poison yet, and so the investigation has to continue to rule out it being hidden anywhere in the house. I'm sorry. I wish it could go faster, but it's impossible. The officers are working as quickly as they can."

"And what is going to happen when they don't find any poison? Will we be able to move back in? Will Mary still be a suspect?"

"Until we can rule her out completely, yes, I'm afraid she will continue to be a suspect. But once Dune House is cleared, you'll be able to move back in right away. I'm hoping it will be by this afternoon, but that's not a guarantee. It's the best that I can do."

"I'll take it." She snapped her fingers as she hung up the phone. To be back home by the afternoon seemed like an impossible dream while surrounded by the four walls of the motel room. But she longed for it. Home.

"Hey, it's me." Mary announced her arrival before she pushed the door open.

"How did it go? Did you find him?" Suzie set her phone down on the table and looked over at her friend.

"Yes, and he admitted that he's her brother." Mary dropped her purse on the same table.

"How did he seem? Resentful? Angry? Do you think it's possible..."

"No, I really don't." She dropped down on to the edge of her bed. "He said their parents are awful people who never did anything to take care of them. If anything, I'd say he was grateful to Cynthia for reaching out to him."

"What about the parents?" Suzie raised an eyebrow. "They could be involved, don't you think?"

"I'm not sure. The way he spoke about them, it seems they were possibly involved in drugs. He hasn't heard from them since they lost the house and disappeared. It's possible, but I don't think it's likely, that they were involved." She rubbed her hand along the curve of her cheek. "So, we're back to square one I think."

"Not quite." Suzie sat down beside her and tossed an arm around her shoulders. "Jason said we might be able to go home this afternoon."

"Home." Mary nodded and a soft smile creased her lips. "That would be nice. No other news?"

"I'm afraid not. We still need to canvas the shops to see if we can find anyone that might have delivered food to the set. Why don't we do a bit of that now? Are you up for it?" She grabbed her phone.

"Sure, hopefully we'll turn up something." Mary slipped her purse back on her shoulder.

~

Just as Suzie and Mary stepped through the door, Paul strode down the hallway towards them.

"Ladies." He smiled at them, but the expression was tight. "How is everything?"

"So far so good. Jason said we might be able to go home this afternoon." Suzie kissed his cheek. She noticed the tension in his jaw. "Is everything okay with you?"

"I just saw Wes in the lobby. He was speaking to Ty, and it didn't look like the conversation was going well." He glanced over his shoulder, then back at them. "I think he might be on to something, but I doubt he's able to share it with us. However, it made me think about just how close Ty and Cynthia were. I wonder if he might be hiding something."

"Like what?" Mary narrowed her eyes. "You think he knows more than he's saying?"

"He's the main actor, the star of this show, if something were to go wrong, say Preston were to be arrested for Cynthia's murder, the entire show might be scrapped before it even gets off the ground. I can't help but wonder if he might be trying to protect Preston to prevent that from happening. I know it doesn't make sense that Preston would kill Cynthia, but I'm guessing that Ty might just be hiding the connection that makes it all make sense. I saw Preston and Ty together twice yesterday and both times their body language told me that the conversation was not friendly."

"Wow, I thought Ty wanted this murder solved as much as we do." Suzie shook her head. "I guess it's possible that he's hiding things. We should talk to him again, maybe this evening? Right now, we're going to check in with the different restaurants and stores to see if anyone delivered anything to the set."

"Oh, I already canvassed most of them. No one had. Here's my list." Paul thrust it out to her.

"Paul, you've been working hard." Suzie looked at all of the places crossed off the list.

"I wish I could say that it led to something good, but so far it's been nothing but dead ends. What about Cynthia's connection to Parish?"

"She definitely had one, she grew up there, and Ryan is actually her brother. But that's as far as that lead got us so far. We don't think Ryan had anything to do with it."

"Though it's still a possibility." Mary raised her hand in the air. "He seems like such a sweet young man though."

"Well, if murderers acted like murderers it would be much easier to catch them." Paul slipped his hand into his pocket. "Here." He held out a folded-up piece of paper to Mary. "This is what I found out about Cynthia's recent movements in town. When I canvassed the restaurants, I asked about her as well. She didn't frequent many of the restaurants, but she did spend a lot of time at the new coffee shop on the Parish border. Maybe she was meeting someone local there? The person I spoke to couldn't recall. Maybe they'll be more talkative with you." He raised an eyebrow.

"Thanks Paul." Suzie wrapped him up in a tight hug. "You're amazing."

"Just be careful." He gave her a quick kiss. "The closer you get to the truth, the more dangerous all of this becomes."

"Yes, he's right." Mary glanced down the hallway. "I'm sure the murderer will do whatever it takes to protect him or herself."

"Then we have to make sure that we get to them first." Suzie met Mary's eyes with a determined stare.

"Absolutely."

"I have to do some work on the boat to make sure it's ready for my next trip. I'll check in with you both later, but if anything comes up, let me know right away." Paul nodded to them, before he turned and headed back down the hallway.

About an hour later Suzie and Mary reached the last name on the list. It was the small Chinese food restaurant that Paul had gotten take-out from the night before, and it was closed.

"I doubt that anyone ordered Chinese and had it delivered. Plus, with all of Cynthia's dietary restrictions, I don't think that she'd be able to eat at a place like this." Suzie crossed the name off the list. "Which leaves us with nothing."

"Another dead end." Mary sighed as she gazed out the window.

"We have to be missing something. The food had to come from somewhere. It wasn't from Dune House, it wasn't from any of the local restaurants. Who else would deliver food?"

"Oh! What about Brad's Brownies?" Mary looked over at her. "I don't think he delivers, but maybe he made an exception."

"That's a good thought," Suzie said. "But are brownies vegan and gluten free?"

"I'm not sure."

"Let's head over there and find out."

~

It was a short drive to Brad's Brownie shop. Although, Mary knew it was a long shot, she hoped that he would have some clue to give them. Brad was busy with someone at the counter when they stepped in. Suzie wandered off to browse while Mary did her best to listen in on the conversation. The person inquired about whether he could mail a package to another state.

"Sure, I can do that. I have to tell you though, the brownies are the best fresh."

"That's all right, I'm sure they'll still like it." The man at the counter, who wore flip-flops and a wide brimmed hat, was obviously on vacation. It wasn't quite warm enough to be called summer yet, and although many people enjoyed the beach at this time, most of the locals waited until it hit the perfect temperature. They concluded their business and Mary smiled at him as he left the shop. She was always especially warm to tourists, not just because the bed and breakfast relied on them, but because the entire town did during the summer season. She knew what it was like to be a new resident in Garber, and though the small town was friendly, the lifetime locals had a special bond. Brad was one of them.

"Hi Brad." Mary leaned against the counter. "How is business?"

"Booming." He studied her for a moment. "I guess I shouldn't ask how things are at Dune House."

"Probably best not to." Mary frowned. "We've had some trouble."

"Yes, I'd say so. You never know what's going to happen when you have all of these out-of-towners staying in your place."

"You're right." Mary nodded. "No one could have expected this, that's for sure."

"Honestly, I'll be glad when all of these Hollywood types clear out of here. I'm never one to decline a customer, but some of them are just far too demanding. Mary, try some of my latest. It's peanut butter spice. Maybe you can guess what the spice is?" He lifted the lid on the sample tray.

"Sure." She smiled, perhaps genuinely for the first time in a few days. When she dropped the piece of brownie in her mouth she was surprised by the taste. There was definitely peanut butter, but there was something else, too.

"Oh? Have you had many orders from our visitors?" Suzie paused in front of the counter and joined their conversation.

Mary couldn't speak as her mouth was full of brownie, but her eyes widened.

"Yes, two too many. The first one was from the woman who died, Cynthia, right?"

"Right." Suzie nodded.

"Well, I can tell you that it wasn't my brownies that poisoned her."

"You can?" Suzie asked.

"Yes, the police believed that Cynthia might have been poisoned by some brownies here so they closed us down for a little while when they searched the store. They didn't find anything, of course."

"When did she order from you?"

"Right after everyone arrived. Apparently, I'm the only place that offers a vegan gluten free treat. Of course, when she placed her order she grilled me about what was really in it, and whether I could prove what ingredients I used. Who asks something like that?" He laughed, then shook his head. "I guess I shouldn't laugh about that."

"It's all right." Suzie patted the back of his hand. "What about the second order? Who did that come from?"

"Actually, I never got his name. But he was just as demanding. He ordered the gluten free vegan brownie bites as well and even asked me to make sure that I gave him an extra box as he was going to share the brownies with a friend. Of course, he didn't pay for an extra box, but I gave it to him anyway. I'm guessing it was a special friend, since he made a special request."

"What request was that?" Mary stepped closer

to the counter with the taste of the brownie still on her tongue.

"He asked that the brownie bites be cut in the shape of a heart. He said he wanted it to send a message. I thought it was weird, since he only wanted two pieces, and two boxes. The brownie bites are quite small." He smiled. "I honestly didn't mind doing that so much. I wished him luck when he picked up the boxes, but he never said a word to me. He wouldn't even look at me. Just walked out, as if I didn't even exist."

"Ouch. That's rather rude." She frowned. "Do you remember what he looked like?"

"He looked like he wore a hat, sunglasses, and a scarf. With his bulky jacket I couldn't even tell you if he was a slender man. But I can say that he wasn't particularly tall or short, just average. Why?"

"Did he pay with a credit card?" Suzie held her breath as she waited for the answer.

"No, I'm afraid not. It was cash, and like I said I never caught his name."

"Is there anything at all you can remember about him? His accent maybe?" Suzie looked into Brad's eyes.

"No, he didn't say much. I will say he didn't seem like he was from around here."

"You did assume he was one of our guests though?" Mary asked.

"Yes, when he opened his wallet he had one of your room keys in it. I didn't see anything else, just that." He shrugged. "I hope he doesn't give you as much trouble as he gave me."

"You said he paid, so was it just his picky request that bothered you?" Mary studied his expression.

"No, it was more than that. I mean he had sunglasses on, but it was as if he looked straight through me. He called his order in ahead and was only here for a few seconds. But in those few seconds, I just felt like I was nothing to him." He lowered his voice. "That probably sounds weird, it's weird for me to say it. I guess, he just unnerved me."

"Interesting." Suzie pulled out her phone. "I wonder if Jason has worked out who it is. Maybe he pulled the phone records, and was able to connect it back to someone staying at Dune House."

"You can suggest it to him." Mary nodded. "Thanks for your time, Brad, sorry that you had to deal with that."

"I'm just sorry about everything that's happened over the past few days. I hope you don't think poorly of me for saying it, but I hope the scandal doesn't affect our summer income."

"I hear you." Suzie sighed as she looked up from her phone. "I'm not sure how Dune House is going to rebound from this, but I hope that it will."

"It will." Mary gave her forearm a light squeeze. "Nothing to worry about. Oh, and it's cinnamon, isn't it?"

"You got it!" Brad grinned. "What do you think? It gives it some pop, right?"

"Yes, it's good." Mary's smile faded some as she thought of what secret ingredient the killer might have added to Cynthia's brownie. As she walked towards the door, the sweet taste in her mouth soured some.

"Who do you think it was that ordered the brownies?" She held open the door for Suzie as they headed back to the car.

"I'm not sure, but I think we're getting closer. It's an odd order to make, don't you think?"

"It's a romantic order." She settled into the car, and smiled as they sped off. "You don't make such special requests unless you're trying to impress or woo someone."

"So, you think?" Suzie glanced over at her. "Marcus?"

"I suppose so. But I don't think poisoning brownies is very romantic."

"No, neither do I." Suzie frowned.

A part of Mary hoped it wouldn't be Marcus. She wanted to believe that the man truly loved his wife, and that he would do anything to please her, not that he would poison a delicious treat.

CHAPTER 12

*S*uzie and Mary headed for the coffee shop. It was their best bet for finding out who Cynthia spent her last moments with. Located at the border of Garber and Parish it was a tiny place, with funky colors and art-filled windows.

"This is the coffee shop." Suzie turned off the ignition and tucked her keys into her purse. "Have you ever been here before?"

"No, it only opened a few months ago and I usually just go to the diner." Mary studied the exterior of the building. "It seems like an artsy place."

"Yes, it does."

"Let's hope we can get more out of them than Paul did." Mary stepped out of the car. Suzie followed after her. When they stepped inside they were greeted by a barista at the counter, and another woman who appeared to be serving as a waitress.

"How can we help you?" The barista smiled.

"I'll take a coffee, with cream and sugar please. Oh, and one of those blueberry muffins." Suzie pointed to the display case with over-sized muffins in it.

"Sure, those are our most popular muffins." As she turned around to prepare the coffee, Suzie continued to talk.

"I guess you heard about the death at Dune House?"

"Sure, everyone has. I wonder how anyone could ever stay there again. I mean, what if it's haunted?" She turned back with the coffee.

"I can assure you, it won't be." Suzie smiled as she accepted the coffee. "Mary, you don't want any coffee?"

"No, thanks." Mary glanced over the photographs hung on the wall. "Who are all of these people?"

"Oh, they're people who come in for our open mics. We have a couple of them a day. Some are poets, some are dancers, singers, whatever."

"Actors?" Suzie looked over at the barista intently.

"Yes, those too." She pointed to one of the photographs.

"There's Cynthia," Mary said.

"Did she perform?" Suzie accepted a plate with a muffin on it.

"Yes, a few times."

"Did she have any fans?" Mary grinned. "Admirers?"

"Uh." She looked up at the ceiling for a moment, then nodded. "Yes actually. I kept his secret for him."

"His secret?" Mary leaned in a little closer, her heart began to pound.

"Mmhm. You know how hard it is for celebrities to go anywhere without being attacked by fans. He wore a hat, and stayed in the back, but I recognized him right away. When I did, he asked me not to tell anyone, because he wanted to see her perform, and he was afraid that if people knew who he was, he wouldn't be able to come back."

"Who?" Suzie's eyes widened.

"Ty Boggs." She grinned. "Right here, in this coffee shop. I guess it's okay to talk about it now, since he's probably not going to come back. He only came to see her." She looked back at the photograph. "I'm not even sure if she knew he was in the audience. I never saw her speak to him."

"What about her husband, Marcus? Did you ever see him around?" Suzie displayed a picture on her phone.

"No." She shook her head as she stared at the screen.

"How about this man?" Suzie scrolled to a picture of Shawn.

"Shawn? Sure, he was in here a lot. Nice guy." She smiled, with just enough color in her cheeks to indicate she might have a crush.

"Was he here when Cynthia was performing?" Suzie tilted her head in the direction of the stage.

"No, not that I saw, anyway. It's always busy during open mics. Oh wait, yes one time. The last time she performed I think. I brought him his coffee, but he didn't touch a sip of it. He seemed a little down, so I brought him a muffin for free. And he wouldn't even touch it." She shrugged. "I guess he didn't like her acting."

"Thanks for your help." Suzie smiled at her.

"Sure, I just hope they figure out what happened to her." She gazed at the stage. "She wasn't the nicest person, but was really talented."

Suzie carried the muffin over to one of the

tables. When they sat down, she pushed the plate towards Mary.

"This is for you."

"Aw, thanks but no thanks, Suzie."

"Mary, you need to eat." She pushed it closer.

"Okay fine, I'll share it with you."

As the two tore apart the muffin, Suzie couldn't help but look in the direction of the stage. Cynthia still had her dreams, and even though she knew that she would never be famous, she still needed to exercise them.

"Do you think she knew that Ty was there watching her?"

Mary's voice drew her from her thoughts.

"Probably, they were friends, right? It wouldn't surprise me if she asked him to come for support."

"Maybe, but he was in the back, disguised, maybe she had no idea." Mary shook her head. "It's amazing the things you learn about people after they're gone."

"Yes, it is. And sometimes it's amazing what you come across about people who are still around." Suzie thumbed through her phone for a moment as she considered whether to update Jason about this information.

She hesitated a moment, then texted him.

Have you looked into Ty?

A few minutes slipped by before he answered.

Can't say.

The text sent a shiver down her spine. Can't say? To her that meant he might have found something out that implicated Ty in the crime. Maybe she was reading too much into it, but surely if there was nothing to it he would have told her it was a dead end. Which made the fact that he was sitting in the back watching Cynthia on stage that much creepier.

A second later another text came through.

You're free to go into the house. Police tape is down, you can use your key to get in.

"Yes!" Suzie jumped up so fast that she almost knocked her coffee over. "Mary, we get to go home!"

"What?" Mary's mouth dropped open. "Now?"

"Yes, now. Jason said we can go any time, it's been released."

"Then what are we waiting for?" Mary reached down and rubbed her ankle. "I can't wait to get my slippers on."

~

*W*ithin minutes Suzie and Mary arrived at Dune House, and Paul arrived right behind them. He'd texted Suzie that he was eager to celebrate with her. Suzie stepped out of the car and gazed up at the building. It looked the same as always, perched above the water like a mansion, but warmer, with welcoming windows and a broad wraparound porch. It was home. When she'd inherited the place from a long-lost uncle she doubted that she would ever consider it home, let alone want to spend the rest of her life in it. But it was home now. She didn't realize how much so, until she'd been told she couldn't stay there. She practically ran up the steps to the porch.

"Wait, wait for me!" Mary laughed as she rushed to catch up with her.

Suzie already had the key in the lock. "I wonder what kind of mess they left in here?" She opened the door, expecting the worst, but everything looked just as it did the day she left. "Wow. No mess so far." She stepped inside, with Mary and Paul right behind her. "Oh, it's so good to be home!" She did a slow spin as she stepped into the foyer of Dune House. "I was beginning to doubt that we would ever see this place again."

"Now that you're back, what are you going to do?" Paul glanced over his shoulder at the door. "Are you going to invite all of the guests back."

"Yes, of course. If they want to come that is. But I think it's important to get things as back to normal as we can. It may take us some time to get to the point that we can feel some relief, but familiar surroundings should help with that."

"I'm not so sure." Mary leaned against the door frame and peered inside. "It's strange, even though I'm back here, it still feels like I'm on the outside for some reason."

"You're not." Suzie grabbed her hand and tugged her inside. "You're right here, with me, where you belong."

"Maybe. But I'm not out of suspicion yet, am I? I mean, the fact that they found no evidence doesn't clear my name. It doesn't cast anyone else as the main suspect, does it?"

"Not just yet, but we're going to get to the bottom of it." Suzie skimmed the living room. "The place is awfully tidy. I expected to find it torn apart."

"I had them put everything back." Jason stepped in behind the three of them. "It took a little guidance and some overtime pay, but they made sure everything was the way they found it."

"Jason, that was kind of you." Suzie met his eyes, and noticed the tension in his expression.

"It wasn't just to save you the trouble." He pulled his hat off his head and looked at Mary. "I knew that when you had the chance you'd want to look over things in the house, and the best way to jog your memory would be to have things remain exactly as they were. I'm hoping you'll think of something, anything, that can help us with the case."

"Like where I hid the poison?" Mary stared at him as she folded her arms across her chest.

"Mary, you know I can't take sides, but I'm certain that you don't think I believe you are responsible for Cynthia's death." He met her eyes. "I don't think that, not even for a second. But I still have to do my job."

"Speaking of the case, Mary and I suspect that the person who purchased the brownies had a romantic interest. Now that we know Ryan was her brother, and not her lover, that centers the suspicion around Marcus, don't you think?" Suzie hoped the question would break the tension between the two.

"Yes, I do, and I am looking into it. However, the problem with Marcus as a suspect is that he is very talkative. I've managed to pin down that he was in conversations with people on the crew for the majority of the time that we believe Cynthia was poisoned. There's a little leeway, but it would be a very tight window. Summer said she should have the final results from the tests on the stomach contents by tomorrow morning. Then at least we may have an idea of what exact poison was used, and that paired with the brownie being the most likely food that was poisoned, could point us in the direction of the murderer. I hope at least."

"Good." Suzie sighed. "Hopefully there will be a record of someone buying the poison."

"We shall see." He glanced over at Mary again. "Anything you can think of, anything you noticed, I'm all ears."

"I know." Mary lowered her eyes. "I wish I could remember more."

"We'll figure it out, Mary." Suzie cast her a bright smile, but the tension had returned.

"Paul." Jason offered him his hand. "I'll talk with you later."

"Yes, let me know if there's anything I can do to help." He shook Jason's hand, before Jason headed out through the door. "I should be going, too. I need to pick up some supplies." Paul gave

Suzie a quick kiss before he walked out after Jason.

"Ugh, I shouldn't have been so cold to him." Mary sighed. "I just don't feel like myself right now."

"It's okay to turn a cold shoulder to the person who can put you in handcuffs. Trust me, I've done it plenty of times." She winked at her friend. "Don't let it get to you, Mary. We're back home, the results are coming in tomorrow, and we're this close to figuring out who did this." She held her fingertips an inch apart.

"Hm." Mary spread her fingers out a bit wider. "Maybe this close."

"Yes, maybe." Suzie grinned. "But soon we'll be this close." She squished her fingertips together.

"I hope so." Mary walked through the kitchen and put a few things back in their places. "I have to admit, they did a very good job of putting everything back. I want to look through all of the rooms and make sure that everything is in place for when the guests return." Mary started up the stairs. Suzie followed after her.

"If they come back." Suzie frowned. "I'm not sure that any will. Like the barista at the coffee shop said, the thought of Cynthia being murdered here might be too uncomfortable for them to move back in."

"Well, hopefully at least a few will." Mary stepped into the first guest room. It was still spotless, but she made sure the pillow was fluffed and the bedspread was smooth.

"I'll help you." Suzie stepped in after her. They went room by room, checking each one over, and wiping up leftover fingerprint dust. "We should make sure to thank Jason for all of this extra effort. They didn't have to put everything back this way."

"No, they didn't." Mary paused outside of Ty's room. "I wonder if he'll come back? What do you think?"

"I'm not sure. I know he values his privacy, and we can give that to him here, but if the story ever breaks on national news, then we might not be able to."

"As long as Preston and Drake continue to protect the location we should be okay."

"Hopefully they will."

Mary began to look over the room, then something caught her eye. "What's this?" Mary crouched down behind the bed. "There's something down here, wedged between the frame and the wall."

"Let me see." Suzie crouched down on the other

side of the bed. "It's shiny." She reached out to see if she could grab it.

"Can you get it?" Mary called out from the other side of the bed.

"No, it's stuck." She sighed and stood up again. "Let's move the bed. Can you get that side?"

"Yes." Mary grabbed her end and braced herself. "Ready?"

"Ready." Suzie nodded, then lifted and slid.

Mary did the same, and soon the bed was a few inches away from the wall. As Mary rubbed her knee, Suzie reached behind the bed and grabbed the silver cylinder.

"How strange." She held it up for Mary to see.

"Oh, that's just Ty's toothbrush." Mary waved her hand. "I guess the police overlooked it since it was stuck back there."

"His toothbrush? Gross." Suzie tossed it over to Mary. But Mary's attention was caught by the sound of someone outside. The cylinder sailed right past her and landed on the floor with a thud. The top and bottom half cracked open, and a small bottle rolled across the floor.

"Oh my!" Mary jumped, then peered at the bottle. "What is that?"

"It's not a toothbrush." Suzie rushed over to take a look.

"It looks like a bottle of oil." Mary reached down to pick up the bottle.

"Mary, don't!" Suzie grabbed her hand just before she could touch it.

"What? Why?" She looked over at her friend.

"Why would he tell you it was a toothbrush if it wasn't?" She stared at her.

"I don't know. You're right. Maybe it's oil of oregano, some people use that for toothaches."

"Maybe, or it could be poison."

"What?" Mary gasped. "You really think so?"

"I think it's a possibility." She narrowed her eyes. "We should call Jason and report this. Obviously, the police missed it."

"Yes, we should." Mary looked towards the window again. "But first I want to know what is going on outside." She stepped closer to the window. A group of photographers and reporters were gathered around the entrance of Dune House. "Uh oh, Suzie, I think we have a problem. I don't think the location of Cynthia's murder is a secret anymore."

"What is it?" Suzie joined her at the window. "Oh no. We'd better go make sure the front is locked up, I don't want any photographs of the interior ending up associated with this."

"All right I'll check the front, you take care of the back." Mary headed for the door. Suzie followed after her. By the time they reached the ground floor, there were cameras at the windows, and sirens in the distance.

"It sounds like Jason is already on his way. Stay away from the windows, Mary."

"I will."

As they locked up all of the entrances, more camera crews arrived. Suzie's cell phone rang. When she saw it was Paul she answered it.

"Hey Paul, it's crazy over here."

"Yes, I noticed. I was trying to get close."

"Don't bother, Jason will have them all cleared out in just a few minutes."

"Suzie, did you leave the back door open?" Mary joined her near the front of the house.

"No. Why? Was it open? I have to go, Paul, I'll call you back when all of this settles down." She hung up the phone and turned to Mary.

"Yes, it was open." Mary sighed. "I guess that one of those photographers got a few snapshots while we were upstairs."

"That's odd." Suzie frowned. "Here comes

Jason." She pulled open the door for him, then closed and locked it behind him. "What's going on? How did word get out?"

"I'm afraid someone at Parish PD might have leaked the information. We're still investigating, but it doesn't matter now, the word is out. I'm not sure that you two will enjoy staying here with all of this craziness."

"Do they know that Ty and the rest of the crew are staying at the motel?" She crossed her arms.

"No, there haven't been any reporters there, so I think it's best if they stay there."

"Yes, unfortunately I agree." She sighed. "Well, at least we're back home." The thought reminded her of what they found upstairs. "Jason, I think your investigators missed something. We found a cylinder wedged behind Ty's bed, and it had a small bottle of liquid in it. I thought it could possibly be the poison you were looking for."

"You did?" He charged up the stairs. "Where is it?"

Suzie and Mary followed after him. "Just inside the first room on the floor. I wouldn't let Mary touch it because I wasn't sure what was inside."

"Where?" He paused in the doorway.

"Just there, on the floor." Mary leaned past him

to point it out, but there was nothing to point at. "What? It was right there." She stepped further into the room.

Suzie dropped down on her knees and peered under the bed. "It didn't roll under here."

"I don't understand, it was there just a second ago." Mary shook her head. "Maybe we kicked it on the way out?" She walked around the perimeter of the room in search of the bottle.

"No, it's gone." Suzie pursed her lips. "Someone came in here and took it." She spun on Jason. "It must have been one of the reporters! Whoever came in the back door."

"Now wait a second, why would a reporter steal something like that?" Jason gazed hard at the floor, when he looked up again, his face was flushed. "There's only one person that would want to steal it, if it was the poison. That would be the killer."

"The cylinder belonged to Ty, I know it did. I found it when I was cleaning his room, and he told me it was a toothbrush holder. How could I be so stupid?"

Mary groaned as she looked away.

"Mary, don't be silly. There's no way that you could have known what it was. Ty is the killer?" Suzie's eyes widened.

"I still have a hard time believing that."

"It doesn't matter what we believe, if that poison was here, then he's the killer." Suzie walked back over to Jason. "You need to go pick him up."

"I'm afraid I can't do that." Jason's eyes narrowed as he scanned the room again. "I have nothing to arrest him for. No evidence. If it was poison that you found, then he is most likely the killer, but the poison is gone. I have no way to prove it was ever here, or even that it was poison. I will go talk to him though." He looked between the two of them. "Not a word about what you found here. If he is the killer, I don't want him to think anyone suspects him. Got it?"

"Yes." Suzie still gazed at the empty floor. "I can't believe we let it disappear."

"It's better that it disappeared than that you or Mary were put at risk." He patted her shoulder. "I'll see what I can find out from Ty." As he spoke Ty's name, Suzie noticed a twitch in his expression. She couldn't place what it meant, but she knew that it meant something.

"Jason, is everything all right?"

"Sure, fine. It's just that he's hired a lawyer, and getting through to him is proving to be quite difficult. Don't worry though, I will question him, it just may take some time."

As he left Dune House he cleared away the reporters, but Suzie knew that it would only be a matter of time before they returned. It was too good of a story for them not to come back.

"Suzie, do you mind if I go out for a bit?"

"No, of course not. Where are you going?" She walked with her out on to the porch.

"I'll let you know. I just want to look into something." Mary gave her a quick hug. "I'll be back soon."

"All right, be cautious. This place is going to be crawling with reporters, and some will do anything to get a story."

"I will be." She met her friend's eyes and held them for a long moment. It meant the world to her that Suzie never once doubted her. But she couldn't let the suspicion that surrounded her become a blemish on the reputation of Dune House.

CHAPTER 13

*M*ary drove towards the motel without a complete plan in mind. As she parked outside, she wished she could call Wes for advice. She was sure that he would know how to get Ty to talk. But he was out of reach, perhaps not just because of the case. As she fiddled with her phone, her stomach flipped with uncertainty. Why, if he doubted her, would she ever want to be with him?

When her phone rang, she jumped so suddenly that she struck her knee on the steering wheel and nearly dropped her phone. As she grabbed it her fingertip slid across the screen. A few colorful words slipped past in the process.

"Mary?"

Wes' voice drifting from the phone silenced her.

161

Had he heard all of that? She blushed as she placed the phone to her ear.

"Sorry Wes, I dropped the phone."

"That's all right. You're not driving, are you?"

"No, I'm parked." She relaxed some as she listened to him speak. It was good to hear his voice.

"I just wanted to check in with you. I know I haven't been around much, and I'm sorry about that. This case is pretty complicated, but I think I'm getting close to the truth."

"I'm glad to hear that. And, it's good to hear from you."

"Are you back at Dune House? I heard it's been cleared."

"No, not at the moment I'm not. I'm at the motel."

"What are you doing there?" His tone shifted from relaxed and warm to tight and stern.

"I was just going to check in with some of the guests."

"Don't. I don't want you anywhere near that motel."

"Why?" Her heart began to pound. What did he know that she didn't?

"I can't tell you, but I need you to listen to me. Stay away from that motel."

"I need this murder to be solved, Wes, just like you have to do what you have to do, I have to do what I have to do. I'll touch base with you later." She hung up before he could argue with her. She didn't want to be talked out of being involved in the case. It was her reputation, her life that hung in the balance, and she wasn't going to risk it just because Wes felt overprotective of her.

After she entered the lobby she headed straight for Ty's room. He might not talk to Jason, but she hoped he would talk to her. After a few light knocks, Ty opened the door.

"Mary." He gestured for her to step in.

"Hi Ty." She searched his expression as he closed the door. "I've been hearing some rumors, and I was hoping you could put them to rest."

"Rumors?" He brushed his hand back through his hair. "What rumors?"

"Just that you and Cynthia might have been more than friends." She raised her hands, palm out. "I'm not here to judge, Ty. But, I don't like to hear lies being passed around."

"Oh Mary, don't think twice about it. Any time I work with a woman, those rumors spread. It's ridiculous, and now with the press in the area it's going to get even worse. Yes, I cared about

Cynthia, she was my friend. But she was also married."

"So, you two were never?" She hesitated to finish the question.

"Mary, you're blushing." He laughed. "No. Never."

"I'm sorry that I asked, I hope I didn't offend you."

"Not at all." He waved his hand.

Although he protested the very idea of romance between himself and Cynthia something about his tone still left her wondering. Why would he hide out in the back of a coffee shop to watch Cynthia if he wasn't interested in her? Perhaps it was a crush that he didn't want to reveal? She realized he was talking to her after he'd already launched into a new subject.

"I'm going to host a small memorial for Cynthia. I know that it may be difficult for you, but I'd like it if both you and Suzie were there." He leaned close to her. "It's going to be short, not much to speak of, but I think it's important that we honor her. I know that as soon as Preston gets the go ahead he's going to want to start filming full force. I'm just afraid that Cynthia's memory is going to get lost in the rush. You know?"

"Yes." She nodded as she studied him. "I think it's very sweet of you to want to do that. I hope that over time the pain you're experiencing lessens."

"I think it will." He rubbed her arm for a moment. "Can I count on you to be there?"

"I'm not sure it's a good idea. I wouldn't want to upset anyone." She frowned as she took a step away from him. "The night should be about Cynthia and it might be hard for people to focus on that if they are looking at me as a suspect. Don't you think?"

"No." He reached for her arm again and held it firmly this time. "I don't think that at all. I think that you should show your face, because you have suffered just as much as the rest of us, perhaps more, since you've been faced with the daunting possibility of going to prison. Why should Marcus be there, free as a bird, when we both know that he should be locked up. Maybe if you show up, it'll shake him up a little bit. I can't stand the thought of him being there, but it wouldn't look right if I didn't invite him."

"Ty, we don't really know that. I mean, I have my suspicions, as do you, but that doesn't make him a murderer. If he did it, there would be evidence, something to prove it. If we're wrong, then we're thinking terrible thoughts about a man who just lost the love of his life."

"The love of his life?" He rolled his eyes. "That man was obsessed with her. Honestly, he still is, even though she's gone. He's not going to let her go, not as long as he can keep riding her coattails to get attention."

"Ty, maybe you should take a moment and consider what you're saying. Yes, Marcus does seem obsessive, but she was also his wife. He wanted to make things work. Now he's grieving her loss. Yes, it's possible that he killed her, but it's just as possible that it could have been someone else."

"Like who?" He shrugged. "Shawn?"

"Maybe. I haven't ruled him out, that's for sure. Why are you so certain it was Marcus?"

"Because he knew." He narrowed his eyes.

"He knew what?" Mary didn't realize that she'd been backing up until her shoulders struck the door.

"That she was having an affair." His expression darkened. "I didn't want to say too much, because I don't want her reputation to be even more harmed by all of this. But, she was cheating on him again. She was my friend, and I don't want it to be splashed all over the news that she was dishonest, that she couldn't be faithful. Is that so much to ask?"

"No, it's not." Her heart softened at the pain in his voice. "She was lucky to have you."

"Maybe." He shook his head. "I wish I had warned her to be careful around him. But I just never thought he would go through with it. Anyway." He took a deep breath, then locked his eyes to hers. "You'll be there tomorrow night?"

"Yes. I'll be there."

"Great." He gave her shoulder a squeeze. "And don't forget, Suzie should be there, too. You should both come early, come by here first, and I can run the service by you."

"I'll make sure we do." As she left the motel, she wondered where Marcus was. Had he fled? Was he holed up in one of the motel rooms? She shivered at the thought of him being anywhere in Garber.

~

Suzie had just set out two plates when Mary stepped through the door.

"Hi there. I made a quick quiche for dinner. I hope you're hungry."

"Yes, I am." She flopped down in an empty chair. "And that smells delicious."

"I just hope it's edible." Suzie laughed. "So, spill. What did you really run off to do?"

"I just spoke with Ty, and he said that he's having a memorial for Cynthia tomorrow night. He wants us to meet him beforehand to go over some things."

"What things?" Suzie raised an eyebrow.

"I'm not sure. Maybe he wants our help setting up." Mary set her purse down on the table and breathed a sigh of relief. It still felt good to be coming home to Dune House instead of the motel.

"Maybe." Suzie frowned as she looked over at her.

"I think it's sweet that he's trying to honor her. It's better than just doing nothing about her death, I mean, with the lack of evidence to convict Marcus, she may never get her justice. At least this way, she's being acknowledged. Her family will have a funeral of course, but this is where she lost her life. It seems fitting that he should want to honor her here as well."

"Marcus? You think it's him now?"

"Yes I think so, especially after what Ty just told me. I don't know with who, but apparently Cynthia was definitely having an affair. Marcus must have found out and decided to kill her."

"The pieces do seem to fit. But Ty couldn't tell you who the affair was with?"

"No, he was pretty guarded about it. He seemed to want to protect her reputation."

"That is sweet of him. I guess we can come up with something. And honestly, Mary this might be the perfect time to take one last shot at the killer. I'm sure Marcus will be there for the memorial." She snapped her fingers. "Yes, this is perfect. I'm not sure how yet, but I think we can do something to shake him up."

"Or ruin a memorial service?" Mary gritted her teeth. "Not exactly the best way to recover our reputation."

"No, it's not. But we will try to keep things under control, and we can't let someone get away with murder."

"You're right." Mary slumped down in the chair and closed her eyes. When she opened them, Suzie had placed a slice of quiche on her plate. "Mm, thank you."

"Eat up. We're going to need our strength."

As Suzie dug her fork through the fluff of cheese on her plate she tried to picture Marcus as a killer. He certainly seemed to be emotionally unstable, though not quite as angry as Shawn. However, did that make him a killer? He had the motive, and the opportunity. If his wife was cheating on him, of course he'd want revenge. But to kill her? That seemed like a huge leap from the way he spoke about her. He seemed to truly love her. But could love get so twisted that he thought no one else deserved to have her?

She and Mary spent the evening reviewing the case and debating ways that they could prove if Marcus was guilty. By the time they both headed for bed, they had an idea of what to do. Suzie could only hope that it would work.

Mary crawled into her own bed, and savored the soft hug it gave her body. As she closed her eyes she thought of the missing bottle in Ty's room. Who had taken it, and why? If it was a reporter she guessed she would hear about it on the news the next day. Or maybe they realized it was something useless, just a bottle of oil or ointment, that had nothing to do with the case. It made her uneasy to think that someone had been in Dune House without her knowing it. But she knew that some reporters would go to any lengths to get a story. She hoped that she wouldn't be that story. It was hard for her to sleep when she imagined the headline splashed across national newspapers. Would they give her a nickname? She shook away the thought. No, she was innocent, and if the plan worked, soon the murderer would be in prison. She thought of Wes, who she'd never checked in with, and wondered whether things would ever be the same between them.

CHAPTER 14

*E*arly the next morning Suzie headed out to hunt down Jason. She wanted to go over a few things with him. However, he was harder to find than she expected. After calling him, and stopping by the station in an attempt to track him down, she decided to do things the old-fashioned way, and drove up and down the quiet streets of Garber. Finally, she spotted it, Jason's patrol car tucked behind some bushes near the old bank. It wasn't occupied anymore, which made it a good hiding place. She guessed he was either napping or setting a speed trap, but when she rapped on his window she realized he wasn't doing either. He had his computer on his lap and the glimpse she caught of the screen revealed that he'd been looking up information about Shawn.

"Suzie!" He looked over at her with surprise. "You shouldn't sneak up on me like that."

"And you shouldn't be so hard to find." She raised an eyebrow.

He stepped out of the car, the door made a loud slam as he closed it.

"Sorry, I missed your call." He flipped his phone from one hand to the other. "I've been trying to find something, anything solid about Cynthia's murder. Why were you trying to find me? Something new?" He looked at her with hope in his eyes.

"Not exactly. Ty is planning a memorial service for Cynthia. I'd guess it would be best if you were there." Suzie did her best to keep her face aligned in a neutral expression. Jason did his best to avoid meeting her eyes.

"You think so?" He squinted at the sun, then glanced at her. "Why is that? Are you planning something?"

She stared at him, slightly surprised. Yes, he was her cousin, they had grown close since she moved into town and turned Dune House into a bed and breakfast, but she hadn't realized that he'd come to know her so well.

"Not exactly." She cleared her throat. "I just

think it would be good. If Marcus and Shawn are both going to be there, fireworks are possible."

"Yes, that's true." He rubbed his chin. "I know about the incident in the lobby. I guess that those two might try to go at it again. You wouldn't do anything to encourage that, would you?"

"I just want the truth to come out, Jason, that's all."

He scuffed his shoe against the pavement and offered a quick look in her direction.

"You're still upset with me, aren't you?"

"The way that Kirk went after Mary, Jason." She frowned.

"I know, I know. But it had to be that way. How would it look if we took it easy on our best suspect?" He shoved his hands in his pockets. "Trust me, it was the last thing I wanted to do, but it wasn't just me involved. With Parish PD breathing down my neck I had to be careful. And, I know Kirk went a little overboard, but to be honest, if it had been any other suspect, I would have told him he did a great job. So why would I send him mixed messages?" He furrowed a brow as he studied her. "Do you think she'll forgive me?"

"Mary?" She laughed and shook her head.

"Mary's already forgiven you. She's the forgiving type. But that doesn't mean you're off the hook."

"Great." He sighed and looked back up at the sky. "So, what will get me off the hook?"

"Finding Cynthia's killer. It's the only definite way to clear Mary's name. As long as the killer is still out there, the question will constantly hang over our heads, over Dune House's reputation. People will still think it's possible that somehow Cynthia's death was our fault."

"I'm trying, Suzie. It's not like I don't want the same thing." His expression grew grim for a moment. "The problem is, the window is so small. The owner of the brownie shop can't identify who purchased the brownies. So here we are, with zero leads, and two promising suspects. I've interviewed Shawn and Marcus multiple times, as well as everyone else on set. Even Ty has made himself available as often as I need. But I can't seem to find that one clue that is going to lead us to the truth. I can't begin to tell you how frustrated I am about it."

"Does Summer know what type of poison was used?"

"Yes, it is odorless and tasteless, but hard to find. You'd have to buy it illegally or work in pest control to get it. She said it's possible that the brownies were laced with poison, but she wasn't able to confirm that. There was no evidence of any poison at the brownie shop."

"So, it wasn't anything that could just be picked up off the shelf?" Suzie shook her head. "That makes it a bit easier, doesn't it?"

"I have the boys back at the station scouring the financial history of everyone that had contact with Cynthia. Hopefully something will pop as the purchase of the poison."

"Good. So, you'll be there this evening?"

"Yes, of course." He studied her for a moment. "I guess even if I tell you not to do whatever you are planning you still will."

"You do know me too well."

"Are you going to tell me your plan?"

"Not just yet." She smiled at him. "But believe me, you'll know it when you see it."

"Great. I think I might need backup." He raised an eyebrow.

"You might." Her voice wavered in a serious tone.

~

*M*ary prepared coffee for herself and Suzie, before she realized that Suzie's purse and keys were gone. "Where did you go so early?" She rubbed the curve of her shoulder and eased her way down into a chair. It was impossible not to be curious about what she might be doing or looking into. But she had to admit that sitting in a warm safe place with fresh coffee was a nice place to be. However, just as she was about to take her first sip there was a knock on the door. She wasn't sure who it could be. Last night she and Suzie had gone down the list of guests and warned them that coming back to Dune House might not be a good idea. She walked over to the door and peeked out through the window along the side of it.

"Ryan!" When she opened the door, he smiled, just a little.

"Sorry to bother you, Mary."

"It's no bother." She studied him. "What do you need?"

"I just wanted to thank you. I've been keeping my secret to myself, and it was nice to have someone else to talk to about it."

"You're welcome, Ryan. Are you going to be at the memorial tonight?"

"What memorial?" Ryan stared at her with wide eyes. "I didn't hear anything about that."

"You didn't?" Mary frowned. "I'm not sure how Ty could have missed contacting you. It's at six-thirty tonight."

"No, I didn't hear a word about it. Why would he leave me out of it?" He narrowed his eyes. "I know I'm a nobody to him, but I mattered to Cynthia."

"Of course you did." Mary surprised herself as she reached out to stroke his cheek. Something about Ryan reminded her of her own son. Perhaps it was the bond between him and his sister. Her children were like that as well. They would always look out for each other. Unfortunately, Ryan could no longer do that for his sister. "More than you will ever know. It must have meant so much to you that she brought you on to the set."

"It did. But now, all I can think is that maybe if I hadn't needed her help, maybe she wouldn't have even taken the job. Maybe she'd still be alive." He reached up to wipe a tear away before it could trail along his cheek. "She didn't need to be here, I did, and maybe if I didn't, everything would be different."

"Don't do that to yourself, Ryan." She clucked her tongue lightly and patted his shoulder. "There is no way that you could have known about any of this. There was no way for you to prevent what happened. Unfortunately, someone terrible did a terrible thing, and now, yes you have to live with the consequences of that for the rest of your life. But you can also know, that your sister loved you, very much. She tried to make things right between you. Even though that might not have been enough, I do hope that you'll find it in your heart to forgive her."

"I do." He closed his eyes for a moment. "I forgave her the moment she came back into my life. But I never had the chance to tell her that. I'm not sure that she knew it. I think maybe she was still trying to make things up to me." He shook his head. "She had such a hard life, and then this is how it ends. Killed by her husband."

"We don't know that for sure, yet." Mary tucked her hands into her pockets as she considered his words. It was easy to assume that Marcus was the killer. He had good reason if he suspected that Cynthia was having another affair. It would be at least the second time she cheated on him, and with his temper, Mary could easily imagine him going after her. But poisoning wasn't an act of rage. It was an act of pre-meditation. One that she wasn't sure Marcus was capable of.

"No, maybe not. But someone did it." He shook his head. "I wish there was a way that I could help her, even now, I feel useless."

"You're not useless, Ryan. You should take the hope she had for you, and make it happen. Hmm?"

"Yes." He sighed as he leaned against the doorway. "I will try. Thanks for telling me about the memorial. I guess I'll see you there."

"Bye Ryan." She waved to him as he walked down the steps into the parking lot. Suzie walked past him, with a brief greeting, then continued straight towards Mary.

"Good morning, Mary."

"Good morning, well almost afternoon now. I can make a fresh pot of coffee if you would like?"

"No thanks, Brad's Brownies should be open by now. I think we should go talk to Brad before it gets too late."

"Okay, let me grab my things." When Mary returned, Suzie was already headed for the car. Mary could see the determination in Suzie's strides. She knew that she was a woman on a mission, and she would do anything to catch Cynthia's killer.

~

On the drive to Brad's Brownies they discussed their plan again.

"All of this hinges on Brad's cooperation. If he won't do it, then we can't do it. I need it to be exactly the same." Suzie tightened her grip on the steering wheel. Her nerves were on edge.

"I think it's a great idea, Suzie. Let's see if we can make it happen." Mary stepped out of the car and headed in the direction of the gifts and goodies shop. Brad did a brisk business during the spring and summer months, as most people loved the fact that the boxes the brownies came in doubled as souvenirs. Each one featured a photograph of a picturesque area in Garber, mostly featuring the beach, but some of the nearby woods, along with the town's name. The box was made of a thin wood and the brownies were wrapped to protect them and prevent them from leaving smudges on the box.

"He's closed." Suzie groaned as she stared at the sign in the window.

"Knock anyway. Maybe he's just doing some work in the back." Mary gestured to the glass door.

Suzie knocked hard several times. After a few

minutes, a light flicked on in the main area of the shop, and Brad made his way to the door.

"What's the trouble?" He opened the door slightly and stared wide-eyed from Suzie to Mary.

"I'm sorry to bother you, Brad, but we need to ask you a favor." Suzie locked eyes with him. "It's going to sound strange, but please, I need you to consider doing it for us."

"What is it?" He pushed open the door and invited them inside. "You two look so upset, what's going on?"

"We believe that someone poisoned the brownies that were ordered from your shop, Brad. We think that's how Cynthia was killed." Suzie let the revelation fall between them, as she knew it would come as a shock.

"But my shop was searched and nothing was found."

"We think they poisoned it after they had bought it."

"That's horrible! Do the police know? Are they going to shut down my shop again?" His eyes fluttered as multiple emotions flashed across his face.

"The police can't prove anything at the moment, I'm afraid, and no your shop won't be in any trouble. But I thought of a plan that might just help us catch the killer. We're going to need your help." She studied him.

"Sure, anything to solve the murder. What is it?"

"I'll need several orders of your two pieces of brownie boxes. I would like about thirty. That should cover it, and I need them by tonight."

"By tonight?" He stared at her. "That's quite a big task. I'm not sure if I can have it ready in time."

"We'll help." Suzie kept her gaze on him. "I believe that only the killer knows what he poisoned, and it will throw him off to see these boxes at the memorial. I'm hoping that he will do something to reveal himself, or perhaps even hesitate to eat the brownies."

"That's a big hope." He frowned. "I'll do it. I won't need any help, thank you though. I can have it ready by six, when I close. My wife gets cross if I'm not home in time for dinner. Would you like me to deliver them on my way home?"

"Yes please, that would be perfect, the memorial starts at six-thirty." Suzie nodded to him. After giving him the delivery details, she and Mary left the shop. Suzie hoped the plan would work. It would rely on the initial shock of the murderer seeing a box of brownies that was the same as the one he'd poisoned, out there in the open. He would know then, that they knew, and that might stir enough fear to be recognizable on his face. Would it be Marcus?

CHAPTER 15

Over the next few hours Suzie and Mary went over every detail of their plan. Then Suzie decided to check in with Jason. However, her calls went straight to voicemail.

"He must be in the middle of something." She hung up the phone and looked at Mary. "Are we ready for this?"

"Yes. We should get going. Ty wanted us there a little early. We have to make sure that we are at the memorial by six so we don't miss the brownies being delivered." Mary smoothed down the milk-white collar of her flower-print dress. It was suitable for a memorial, with just enough color to indicate a sense of celebration of life. In contrast, Suzie's black dress seemed drab. She tugged at the skirt and smoothed it down.

"Maybe I should change."

"Is there time?" Mary glanced at her watch.

"No, there's really not. Let's just go. We don't want to delay anything. As long as this is perfectly timed it will all go smoothly." Suzie straightened her skirt one last time then snatched up her purse, and a flower on a pin and put it in her pocket. She would pin the pink flower to her dress before the memorial.

"Are you sure about this, Suzie? What if we're wrong? What if the killer isn't even at the memorial?" Mary's eyes creased with concern. "I mean it seems a little twisted to serve the very food that killed Cynthia at her memorial."

"Then we've blown it. But this is our last chance, Mary. This is the only thing that we can do to try to solve the murder."

"All right, let's go then." Mary grabbed her purse, and her keys. "I'll drive."

As Suzie followed her out the door of Dune House, it was hard for her not to think about the last time she'd seen Cynthia there. She was a sweet woman underneath, she guessed. But she hadn't shown it during her stay there, and her treatment of Mary had made all of Suzie's protective instincts ramp up. She'd wished ill will on the woman. She'd given her a tongue-lashing in the safety of her own mind, and now she was going to her memorial. It did feel wrong.

They sat in silence on the way to the motel. Mary focused on driving. When she neared the parking lot, she glanced over at Suzie.

"It's nice of Ty to arrange this. Don't you think?"

"I do." Suzie hesitated. "But what about the cylinder we found?"

"What about it?" She shrugged. "It probably had nothing to do with the case."

"Then why would someone take it." Suzie narrowed her eyes. "It seems so odd."

"I'm guessing it was one of the reporters. Maybe they thought it had something to do with the murder, or maybe they knew that it belonged to Ty. If so then it will end up on the internet for some astronomical price." She parked in front of the motel.

"Yes, I guess you're right."

When they reached Ty's room, he answered the door after the first knock. He was dressed in a three-piece suit which was a combination of rich black, and deep maroon. His hair was combed, and he was clean-shaven. It seemed to Suzie as if he'd made quite an effort to look nice for the memorial.

"Ladies, I'm so glad that you could make it. Come in, please." He held the door open for them as they stepped inside.

"Where is everyone else?" Suzie paused a few steps past the door.

"Oh, they'll be along." He pulled the door shut behind Mary. "I thought it would be good for the three of us to have a moment to talk about the memorial."

"We can talk after." Suzie's heart began to pound. She couldn't put her finger on it, but something did not feel right. "We should be going, we have some things to do before the service." She gazed at him for a long moment. Something about his demeanor was off. His smile was lopsided, and his body language was tight, controlled. She recalled Mary telling her about Ryan's insistence that he knew nothing about the memorial. Jason didn't either, until she told him. Who exactly had Ty invited if he left out the victim's brother and the local police?

"Oh, please don't rush off. I just want to make sure that everything goes off without a hitch. I don't want anyone losing their temper. I'm certain that Marcus will go after Shawn again. That's why I have this." He pulled something out of his pocket. It was small, metal, and odd looking.

"Is that a taser?" Mary stepped forward, and as she did, Suzie moved closer to her. "Why do you have that?"

"It just causes a small disabling shock. If Shawn gets out of control, then I'll be able to stop him before things get messy. Or maybe I'll use it on Marcus, to get him to confess." He laughed, an awkward laugh, that left Suzie even more confused. "It doesn't hurt much at all, do you want to try it?" He jabbed it in Mary's direction.

Mary lunged back before the taser could make contact. Suzie stepped in front of her and glared at Ty.

"Are you drunk?"

"Maybe." He shrugged.

"I don't think that's a good idea, Ty. Jason will be there. He'll be able to handle Marcus if he loses it. Just leave that here, all right?"

"I'm afraid I can't do that." He gripped the taser a little tighter. "Ladies, I'm not sure that you will understand this, but some things just have to be done."

"Things? If Shawn is guilty then he will have his trial and we will get to the bottom of everything that happened. But you can't take justice into your own hands." Suzie narrowed her eyes. "Leave it here, or I'm going to tell Jason about it. He won't want any other weapons there."

"Will you now?" He chuckled, and a strange light entered his eyes. It took her breath away to see it. "Are you going to tell on me, Suzie?"

"Mary, open the door." Suzie took a step back.

"Go on, Mary, open the door." Ty winked at her as she reached for the knob. When she twisted the handle, it wouldn't budge.

"I can't, it's locked." Mary jiggled the knob but it wouldn't give.

"It can't be locked on the inside." Suzie turned to face her, and in that moment she saw that the door handle was not like the rest of the handles in the motel. It had a keyhole on the inside.

"I asked the manager of the motel to replace it for me. You see, I became a little particular about my room. I decided that I would like to be able to lock it from the inside and the outside. It's funny, some people would find that strange, but when you have enough money, they'll do anything to please you. Have a seat, ladies." He gestured to two wooden chairs near a small table.

"No, thanks." Suzie narrowed her eyes. "We

need to leave or we'll miss the memorial. If we don't show up, then what will people think?"

"A memorial for that harlot?" He laughed and pointed to the chairs again, then waved the taser "Let's just get along, I don't want to have to leave any marks. There's nothing to miss. There is no memorial. No one will be looking for you."

Mary grabbed Suzie's hand as her heart pounded. "Let us go, Ty, you have no reason to keep us here. Whatever you did, your fame, your money, it can get you out of it. But not if you add two bodies to the list."

"I have every reason to keep you here!" The anger in his voice was evident as it bounced off the walls of the room. "Sit down!" He thrust the taser towards Mary's neck, but did not touch it to her skin. Mary sank down in one of the chairs, Suzie dropped down into the other.

"I had it planned out well, I thought. Everything was coming together perfectly, I poisoned her shortly after lunch. We went somewhere near the set by ourselves and pretended that we were going to rehearse my lines. It all worked perfectly. But then the police shut down Dune House before I could get back into my room. I tried to get to my room before you two were allowed back in, but I wasn't fast enough. So, you found my stash. And it was then I knew, you two would figure it out eventually. I managed to get the bottle back, but I knew that wouldn't help in the long run." He paced back and forth for a few moments, then turned to look at them. "I never saw this plot twist in my life. I never saw myself becoming a murderer, but when it happened, it was as if I finally stepped into my greatest role. I became, me. Understand?" He laughed. "It was beautiful."

"Ty, what did you do?" Mary's voice was soft as she spoke, but Suzie could detect the hardness underneath. She was determined to get through to Ty, even if it meant pretending to be kind. "Whatever it is, Suzie and I can help you."

"No, you can't." He paused in front of them. "Have you ever been in love, either of you?"

"I was married…"

"I didn't ask that. I asked you if you'd ever been in love. That maddening, addictive kind of love that takes your breath away?" He looked between them.

"No." Mary finally answered, and shook her head. "I don't think so."

"Maybe once." Suzie bit into her bottom lip.

"You would know if you were. I never believed it was possible, until Cynthia. She became like the air to me, like I needed to be near her in order to breathe." He took a long slow breath. "I thought, my life was going to change. Finally, I was going to be the lucky one. But she didn't agree. She told me she wanted to break things off, that she wanted to work it out with Marcus. Can you believe that nonsense?" He chuckled. "That man is barely more than a potato, but she felt as if she owed him, for staying by her side after everything that happened with Shawn. Ridiculous. I needed her. I had to have her."

"So, you killed her?" Mary broke in with a soft gasp. "Because she wouldn't be with you?"

"Honestly, I wasn't sure if I could go through with it. It seemed so Romeo and Juliet to me, you know? Just a bit too dramatic. But, I thought, we could go out together. She'd take a bite, then I'd take a bite, and it would all be over. We'd be together, forever." He closed his eyes, but just for a moment.

"But you're still here." Suzie stared at him as her heart slammed against her chest. "You didn't take that bite."

"No. I didn't. It turns out, I don't really want to die. And, it's funny, when she ate that brownie, like it was nothing, like she had no idea that it was the last bite she'd ever take, it turned me off. I guess I expected her to be smarter, or more intuitive or something. But instead, she popped that hunk of sugar in her mouth and sucked it down without a second thought. She didn't even notice the poison. All of a sudden I realized, she wasn't this magical being that had been brought into my life, she was just a woman, a soon to be dead woman at that point." He shrugged. "So, I let her eat the other piece, too."

"You could have gotten her help." Mary's eyes widened. "They might have been able to save her!"

"No, I would have had to admit what I'd done, and of course, I couldn't do that." He glanced at his watch. "Oops, it's time for my debut." He winked at both of them. "I'm sure there will be plenty of cameras around to capture the moment that I offer a heartfelt speech about the great loss of my friend, Cynthia, and just how heartbroken I am. Every reporter in town will be there, I made sure to get their attention. I should be fielding movie offers by later tonight. I guess that's something to celebrate." He straightened his tie. "You two sit tight, I'll deal with you when I get back."

As he stepped through the door Suzie thought about lunging for him. She thought perhaps she could wrestle him to the ground, but the more she thought about it, the more she realized that it was not a wise move. If she gave Ty a reason to believe that they would be troublesome then he might just decide to kill them right then. Maybe, he expected them to attack and that would launch him into his murderous spree. Instead, she remained still and silent until she heard the door close and lock. There was no way out. The windows were reinforced glass and bolted. It should have been illegal, considering fire safety. Maybe he'd made that request of the motel as well. Maybe he'd ensured that the room would be turned into a cage, as he suspected he might need it. Suddenly, the door swung open again, and Ty stepped back inside. He slammed the door shut and walked towards them.

"So sorry, I think I need a little extra reassurance that you two are not going to cause me any more trouble." He pulled out two lengths of rope and began tying Mary down to a chair. "Don't." He shot a look in Suzie's direction. "If you take one step towards me, I will inject her with the same poison I killed Cynthia with. It works much faster when injected."

"You wouldn't." Suzie stared at him. "You're bluffing!"

"Do you want to find out?" He tightened the ropes enough that Mary had to hold back a groan.

"It's okay, Suzie." She breathed past the pain.

He turned to Suzie next. She considered putting up a struggle, but she couldn't risk the possibility that he really did have the poison.

"There, that's better." He patted her knee. "Don't bother screaming either. These rooms are quite sound proofed, and I made sure that the rooms all around mine would be empty, for privacy, you know. Can't be too careful." He winked at them, then stepped out the door again.

"Suzie, we have to get out of here." Mary shifted in the ropes that tied her hands. She glanced past her friend, to the window. "Maybe if we throw the table at it."

"No, it won't work." Suzie took a deep breath as she tried to work her own hands free. They were too far apart to be able to aid each other with the ropes. Mary began to wiggle back and forth in her chair in an attempt to creep towards Suzie.

"Careful Mary, if you tip, you could get hurt." Suzie watched her with wide wary eyes.

"We have to do something or we're going to be stuck waiting here until he gets back, and then you know what will happen." Mary closed her eyes.

When she opened them again, she looked towards the bedside table. "Shouldn't there be a phone?"

Suzie looked in the direction of the table as well, but there was nothing on it, and where a cord should have been the space was empty. He definitely planned all of this out.

"How did we not see this coming?"

"He's a great actor." Mary sighed. "I guess if you're a good actor, you can get away with any lie."

"Yes, I guess so. It doesn't make me feel any better about missing it though. I thought Ty was a nice guy."

"Maybe he was at one point." Mary shook her head. "Maybe something just snapped inside of him."

"Maybe." Suzie frowned, then stretched her wrists against the ropes again. "I think he must have been a boy scout. These knots are impossible."

"We have to try to stay calm. I'm sure that someone will notice that we're not at the memorial. Right?"

"If there is a memorial. Remember what Ryan told you? He wasn't invited. I'm willing to bet it might just be a press conference, where Ty gets to make his speech and gain the sympathy of the entire country."

"You may be right." Mary scuffed her feet against the carpet. "If I push back I can tip this chair over."

"Don't, you'll hit the counter." Suzie looked past her at the small kitchen counter. "You could split your head open."

"Okay, any ideas?" The exasperation in Mary's voice indicated she was on the verge of panic.

"There's a sprinkler system, right? Every motel has one. If we trigger it, then it should set off the fire alarm. They will have to do a room by room search to ensure that everyone is evacuated."

"But that will take hours, and how are we going to get up there to trigger the sprinklers?" Mary stared across the table at her.

"You asked for ideas, not good ideas." She closed her eyes and forced a laugh.

"Ugh, Suzie." She fluttered her eyes, then gazed up at the ceiling. "If only one of us was a smoker we might just have a lighter on us."

"Nope, nothing." She shifted in her chair and suddenly felt the rub of something in her pocket. It was the pin with the flower on it that she'd intended to put on her dress when they arrived at the memorial. Since it was in her skirt pocket she was able to bunch up the material enough to drag the pocket close to her fingertips. As she worked the pin free, she gritted her teeth.

"What are you doing?" Mary peered at her.

"I'm not sure. I have a pin in my pocket, I thought maybe I could use it for something."

"A pin isn't going to cut through thick rope." Mary frowned.

"No, it's not." She finally managed to get it free and pinched it between her fingertips. "But it's all I have."

"Maybe you could use it to etch a message into the chair. Maybe someone will notice it, and find out what Ty did." Mary's voice raised a little. "At least, he might be caught then."

"Mary, you're talking as if we're already dead. We're going to get out of here, I know it."

"No, you don't know that." Mary rocked her chair again, back and forth.

"We have to find a way out."

"Suzie, it's too late." Mary tilted her head in the direction of the doorknob as it began to twist. Her stomach twisted much faster and harder. The only person that could be opening it was Ty, which meant that he'd come back to finish them off.

CHAPTER 16

As the door began to open, Mary closed her eyes. She didn't want to see Ty's smile.

"Wes!" Suzie's exclamation caused Mary's eyes to fly open. She saw Wes move towards her, and in that moment it was the most beautiful sight she could have ever seen.

"Wes, hurry, it's Ty, and he's coming back for us."

"No, he's not sweetheart." He ducked behind her and freed her from the ropes, then he moved on to Suzie's hands. "Are you both okay? He didn't hurt you?" His eyes lingered on Mary.

"No, we're okay. But we should go, Wes, he's coming back." She stood up from the chair and did her best to ignore the quake in her legs.

"No, he's not. He's in the back of Jason's patrol

car. He's not going anywhere." He wrapped his arms around her. "I'm sorry you went through this. I'm sorry that I didn't figure everything out before he put his hands on you."

"How did you figure it out?" Suzie stood up and rubbed her wrists.

"I've had my eye on Ty for quite some time. When I was doing research on him I realized he was single. He wasn't even dating around. I thought that was strange. As popular and well-liked as he is, I couldn't figure out why he wouldn't be dating. When I dug deeper into his past I found out he has an old buried charge for stalking. I still didn't quite grasp it, until Jason told me about the bottle you two found in Dune House. We had dogs in there, searching for any trace of the poison that was used to kill Cynthia, but we didn't find anything. It occurred to me that if he stored the poison in a bottle of scented oil there was a good chance the dogs wouldn't be able to detect it."

"You genius!" Mary cupped his cheeks and planted a heavy kiss on his lips.

He laughed as he pulled away from her.

"If I was a genius it wouldn't have taken me this long to get here, and by the way, your trick is the real reason that Ty was caught."

"What do you mean?" Suzie raised an eyebrow.

"When the brownies were delivered to the press conference, Ty knocked it out of Brad's hand and backed away. I think he expected it to be poisoned. I acted as if I knew everything there was to know and had evidence to back it up. He broke down and admitted to everything." He sought Mary's eyes with determination. "Mary, I never wanted you to get caught up in any of this."

"I know you didn't." She caressed his cheek and thought about all of the moments she wondered if he'd given up on her. "I'm sorry that I ever doubted you."

"There was no reason to." Jason stepped into the room, followed by Paul. Suzie rushed into Paul's arms, and as he held her close, Jason continued. "Mary, if it wasn't for Wes, you would have been in handcuffs. He fought hard to keep you from being arrested. Honestly, he went further than I could have."

"Wes? Is that true?" She looked into his eyes.

"Yes, of course it is. When I was assigned to the case, I knew it would be a conflict, but I thought the best way to protect you would be to investigate the murder myself. I would do anything to protect you, Mary." He held her a little tighter against his chest.

"But your job, it's so important." She frowned. "I would never want you to put it at risk."

"I love my job, Mary, it's what I've always wanted to do. But I wouldn't even hesitate to give it up in order to protect you." He brushed her hair back behind her ear and gazed at her. "Never forget that."

The two shared a lingering kiss. When they finally broke apart, Mary's cheeks were bright pink. "Maybe it's time we gave Cynthia the memorial she really deserves, and hopefully her brother Ryan some peace."

Suzie led the way out of the motel room. Outside they were greeted by cameras, and reporters eager for a story. But this time, they weren't going to get some story, they were going to get the truth.

The End

ALSO BY CINDY BELL

DUNE HOUSE COZY MYSTERIES

Seaside Secrets

Boats and Bad Guys

Treasured History

Hidden Hideaways

Dodgy Dealings

Suspects and Surprises

Ruffled Feathers

A Fishy Discovery

Danger in the Depths

BEKKI THE BEAUTICIAN COZY MYSTERIES

Hairspray and Homicide

A Dyed Blonde and a Dead Body

Mascara and Murder

Pageant and Poison

Conditioner and a Corpse

Mistletoe, Makeup and Murder

Hairpin, Hair Dryer and Homicide

Blush, a Bride and a Body

Shampoo and a Stiff

Cosmetics, a Cruise and a Killer

Lipstick, a Long Iron and Lifeless

Camping, Concealer and Criminals

Treated and Dyed

A Wrinkle-Free Murder

SAGE GARDENS COZY MYSTERIES

Birthdays Can Be Deadly

Money Can Be Deadly

Trust Can Be Deadly

Ties Can Be Deadly

Rocks Can Be Deadly

Jewelry Can Be Deadly

Numbers Can Be Deadly

Memories Can Be Deadly

Paintings Can Be Deadly

Snow Can Be Deadly

A MACARON PATISSERIE COZY MYSTERY SERIES

Sifting for Suspects

Recipes and Revenge

Mansions, Macarons and Murder

NUTS ABOUT NUTS COZY MYSTERIES

A Tough Case to Crack

A Seed of Doubt

HEAVENLY HIGHLAND INN COZY MYSTERIES

Murdering the Roses

Dead in the Daisies

Killing the Carnations

Drowning the Daffodils

Suffocating the Sunflowers

Books, Bullets and Blooms

A Deadly Serious Gardening Contest

A Bridal Bouquet and a Body

Digging for Dirt

CHOCOLATE CENTERED COZY MYSTERIES

The Sweet Smell of Murder

A Deadly Delicious Delivery

A Bitter Sweet Murder

A Treacherous Tasty Trail

Luscious Pastry at a Lethal Party

Trouble and Treats

Fudge Films and Felonies

Custom-Made Murder

WENDY THE WEDDING PLANNER COZY MYSTERIES

Matrimony, Money and Murder

Chefs, Ceremonies and Crimes

Knives and Nuptials

Mice, Marriage and Murder

ABOUT THE AUTHOR

Cindy Bell is the author of the cozy mystery series Dune House, Sage Gardens, Chocolate Centered, Macaron Patisserie, Nuts about Nuts, Bekki the Beautician, Heavenly Highland Inn and Wendy the Wedding Planner.

Cindy has always loved reading, but it is only recently that she has discovered her passion for writing romantic cozy mysteries. She loves walking along the beach thinking of the next adventure her characters can embark on.

You can sign up for her newsletter so you are notified of her latest releases at http://www.cindybellbooks.com.

Made in the USA
Columbia, SC
18 June 2020

11370332R00117